THE IMPETUOUS DUCHESS

The Duke of Warminster was uncontrollably angry. First the silly young twit had lied her way into his carriage—forcing him to drive halfway across Scotland with her. Then, when the carriage overturned and he was injured, she lied again and told the Scottish couple who gave them shelter that she and the Duke were married.

Their hostess saw through the story in a minute. With a twinkle in her eye she sought to acquaint the Duke and his "bride" with an odd statute of Scottish law making anyone who uttered a declaration of marriage before witnesses legally wed. The Duke was speechless. Could it be that he and this mindless little fool were actually married?

Bantam Books by Barbara Cartland
Ask your bookseller for the books you have missed

The Impetuous Duchess

BARBARA CARTLAND

THE IMPETUOUS DUCHESS
A Bantam Book / April 1975

Bantam Books are published by Bantam Books, Inc. Its trade-
mark, consisting of the words "Bantam Books" and the por-
trayal of a bantam, is registered in the United States Patent
Office and in other countries. Marca Registrada. Bantam
Books, Inc., 666 Fifth Avenue, New York, New York 10019.

PRINTED IN THE UNITED STATES OF AMERICA

Author's Note

"Marriage by Declaration" before witnesses, or Irregular Marriage, was legal in Scotland until the Act was repealed in 1949.

Napoleon Bonaparte's action at the renewal of hostilities in 1803 in treating ten thousand English tourists in France as prisoners of war was condemned at the time as a violation of all civilised behaviour.

The Impetuous Duchess

Chapter One

1803

"Excuse me, Your Grace."

The Duke of Warminster raised his eyes from the book he was reading while he ate.

Standing in the doorway of the private parlour of the Posting-Inn was his second coachman, somewhat awkwardly twisting his velvet cap in his hands.

"What is it, Clements?" the Duke enquired.

"Th'weather be a worsening, Your Grace, and Mr. Higman thinks it's be unwise to tarry long. He learns 'tis some distance to the next Inn where we could change horses or rest for th'night."

"Very well, Clements. I will not be more than a few minutes," the Duke replied.

The second coachman bowed and went from the parlour.

The Duke closed his book reluctantly and picked up the glass of inferior wine which was the best the Inn could provide.

The meal had not been a good one—the mutton had been tough and there had been no choice of dishes.

But what could be expected in such a wild part of the country, with at this time of the year few travellers of any importance?

It had been, as the Duke was well aware, an unusual procedure for someone of his importance to journey to Scotland when there was still snow on the ground and the weather, to say the very least of it, was uncertain.

But he had been extremely anxious to discuss with the Duke of Buccleuch at Dalkeith Palace some manuscripts he had recently discovered at Warminster which linked their families in the reign of Henry VIII.

He had therefore braved the elements and been rewarded for his courage by having what had been to all intents a smooth journey to Edinburgh.

He had stayed at Edinburgh Castle for some nights and then proceeded to join the Duke of Buccleuch at his Palace for a number of long, earnest, and erudite discussions which they had both much enjoyed.

"Warminster is far too young," the Duchess of Buccleuch had said tartly to her husband, "to spend his time poring over dusty volumes when he might be looking at pretty women."

"His Grace does not find contemporary socialites as alluring as past history," her husband replied with a smile.

The Duchess however had done her best to interest the Duke of Warminster in their youngest daughter, a pleasant young woman with considerable talents in music and painting.

The Duke, though extremely polite, had made it quite clear that his only interest in visiting Dalkeith Palace was to talk with its owner.

He had set out on his homeward journey well satisfied with the results of his visit, and convinced that, as it was now the beginning of April, Spring was in the air.

But during the last few days there had been unprecedented gales which had made the Duke's carriage rock precariously on the rough roads, made hard and slippery with recent frosts.

However the Duke was too immersed in his books to notice such minor discomforts.

He had stayed at Thirlstone Castle with the Earl of Lauderdale and for a few nights at Floors, a magnificent building erected in 1718 by Vanburgh.

Now he had no more visits to make, and there were no more convenient hosts to offer him hospitality before crossing the Border.

As was usual on such occasions, the Duke's servants grumbled and complained at the discomforts of the journey far more than their employer.

It was true that the second coach, carrying the Duke's valet, also contained besides his luggage certain comforts that were not accorded to lesser personages.

His Grace for instance always travelled with his own crested linen sheets, soft lambswool blankets, and his special goose-feathered pillows.

There were also some bottles of excellent claret and brandy, which despite the jolting they had received were considerably more palatable than anything that could be purchased at the local Inns.

It was unfortunate that, when His Grace had stopped at *The Grouse and Thistle* at midday, the second travelling coach had fallen behind.

This was doubtless because Higman, the Duke's first coachman, had insisted on taking all the best posting-horses for himself, which meant that only very inferior horseflesh had been left for the second coach.

"I tells His Grace afore we starts," the third coachman said bitterly, "that us couldn't rely on obtaining decent animals in a heathen barbaric country like Scotland. But would his Nibs listen? No!"

It was a statement the other servants had heard a hundred times since they had set out from Warminster.

The fact that the Duke himself had journeyed to Scotland on his yacht before joining his coaches at Berwick-on-Tweed had done nothing to mollify the coachman's resentment.

Inferior animals though the horses might be, they certainly seemed impervious to the roughness of the roads and the sharpness of the winds, which would undoubtedly have disturbed and perhaps incapacitated

horses from the South, which were not used to such
weather.

As he finished his wine the Duke rose from the table
at which he had been sitting and crossing the room
picked up the fur-lined cloak in which he always travelled.

He was holding it in his hands as the door opened
again, and a mob-capped maid who, he thought, must
be the daughter of the landlord bobbed him a curtsy.

"Oi've a request t'make of Your Grace," she said in
a broad Scots accent.

"What is it?" the Duke asked, putting on his cloak
with some difficulty in the absence of his valet.

"There be an elderly lady, Your Grace, who begs
ye'll be kind enough ta allow her ta travel with ye ta
the next Posting-Inn. She's had an accident with her
coach and there be nae way for her ta reach tha without the help o'Your Grace."

The Duke paused in the process of buttoning his
cloak.

He had a rooted objection to travelling in a coach
with anyone, let alone a stranger.

He liked reading while he was travelling, or simply
contemplating quietly in silence the many projects on
which he was engaged on his Estates.

The mere idea of having to make conversation, or to
have someone chattering to him on the long miles that
he must journey before he reached the Posting-Inn,
filled him with dismay.

"Surely," he said tentatively, "there must be some
other way in which this lady can reach her destination?"

"Nay, Your Grace," the maid answered. "Th'stage-
coach only comes through here once a week and we'll
not see it agin 'til after tha Sabbath."

The Duke longed to allege that there was no room
for a passenger in his coach, but he knew that the well-
sprung, recently built vehicle had evoked interest and
admiration wherever it had appeared.

Doubtless the elderly lady in question had already

inspected its interior before asking him if he would give her a lift.

It was therefore with a sigh of exasperation which he could not repress that he replied:

"Very well. Will you tell the lady I am pleased to offer her a seat in my carriage, but that I am departing immediately?"

"Oi'll tell th'lady, Your Grace," the maid said, and curtsying sped from the parlour.

The Duke was about to follow her when the landlord appeared with his bill. This was something the Duke had forgotten.

Whenever he travelled without a courier, his valet invariably settled all accounts. The Duke himself was never bothered with bills or the necessity for carrying money.

Fortunately he had a few golden sovereigns in his waist-coat pocket, and he placed one on the salver which the landlord handed him, waving aside the suggestion that there should be any change.

He had obviously overpaid, for the landlord was profuse in his gratitude, bowing and scraping—in an excess of goodwill, as he escorted the Duke to his carriage and expressed many regrets that he had not been previously advised of His Grace's visit so that better fare could have been provided.

The Duke closed his ears in a manner that he had found most convenient when he did not wish to listen.

Yet by smiling pleasantly at the man when he finally reached the door of the carriage he left the landlord with the conviction that he had been extremely pleased with his reception.

A blustery wind blowing round the side of the Inn almost swept the Duke's hat from his head. Holding it firmly in place he stepped hastily into the carriage.

Already seated in the far corner of the coach was the figure of a woman wearing a dark travelling-cape, the hood trimmed with fur pulled forward, leaving her face in shadow.

5

She was covered with a fur rug and as the Duke seated himself the second coachman tucked another round his legs. He felt beneath his feet a foot-warmer which had been refilled at the Inn.

"Good-evening, Ma'am," the Duke said to the lady beside him. "I regret to learn there has been an accident to your coach. I am glad that I can be of service in conveying you further on your journey."

"Thank you."

The words were spoken in a low and what seemed a quavering voice.

His companion, the Duke decided, was obviously very old, in which case she would probably sleep and would therefore not disturb him.

To make quite sure that she was aware he did not intend to converse as the horses turned out of the yard and onto the open road, he opened his book ostentatiously.

There was no doubt the wind had risen a great deal since the morning and now it beat ferociously against the carriage, so that if the vehicle had not been so well made, the windows would undoubtedly have rattled.

The Duke settled himself comfortably, feeling that if anyone could get up a good speed out of the four horses pulling the carriage, it would be Higman.

At the same time he hoped the second carriage would not be too long delayed. He was well aware, when it came to spending a night at a local Inn, how indispensable his valet was to his comfort.

Trusgrove had been with him ever since he was a boy, and in some magical manner he could always conjure up hot water, bed-warmers, and even an edible dinner however unprepossessing their accommodation might appear.

The Duke stopped thinking of his valet in the second coach. He suddenly realised they must have travelled for some miles and yet his lady passenger had neither moved nor spoken.

He told himself that this was exactly what he wanted, that it was a source of real satisfaction, so that he would not regret having done a kindly action in giving her a lift.

At the same time he could not help feeling curious as to who she might be, and he found himself ostensibly reading a whole page of his book and yet not taking in a word.

A sudden fresh gust of wind gave him an excuse for saying aloud:

"Surely, Ma'am, this is unprecedented weather for the time of the year?"

"Yes . . . it is."

The words were low and again the voice sounded quavery.

It was obvious, the Duke thought, that the lady had no wish to talk, and he told himself with a smile that for once he had found someone who was more of a recluse than he was himself!

He turned back the page of his book and began to read it again.

As he did so they came to a sudden bend in the road, and what must have been a recent fall of snow caused the coach to check for a moment.

Then it slipped sideways so that the lady was flung from the other side of the coach against the Duke.

He put out his hands to save her from falling and as he did so, the hood of her driving-cape fell back a little to reveal two large, bright eyes in a small, heart-shaped face.

The Duke stared in astonishment.

This was no elderly woman but a young girl, very young it appeared! She quickly pulled the hood back into place and slipped back into the corner of the carriage, but the Duke had already seen her.

"I was told," the Duke said slowly, "that it was an elderly lady who required my assistance."

There was a moment's hesitation and then the girl, for the Duke was convinced she was nothing more, said almost defiantly:

"I had a feeling you might . . . refuse to take me unless you thought I was old and in need of . . . help."

7

"You are quite correct in your supposition," the Duke said. "But now that it is no longer possible for you to continue with your pretence, perhaps you would tell me why you are travelling alone?"

In answer his companion pushed back the hood to reveal vividly red hair which curled in a rather unfashionable manner over her head.

Her eyes were a very dark grey-green, almost the colour of the sea, and even in the dimness of the coach the Duke could see that her skin was white, clear, and translucent.

She smiled at him and said gaily:

"I am glad I no longer need to use that quavering voice. But it did deceive you, did it not?"

"It did indeed," the Duke replied. "But then why should I suspect that what I had been told was untrue?"

"I was so afraid that you would refuse to help me," his companion said. "But now we are at least three miles on our way and there is nothing you can do about me."

Her tone was so complacent that the Duke could not help saying:

"I could of course set you down on the roadside!"

"Leaving me to freeze to death in this weather?" the girl asked. "That would be extremely ungentlemanly!"

The Duke looked at her, taking in the small, pointed face and the clear-cut features.

She was not beautiful, he decided, but she was extremely pretty and there was a fascination in the way she smiled and in the sparkle of her eyes that he had not encountered in other young women.

More than anything else she was obviously a Lady of Quality, and with a sense of some dismay he asked:

"I think it would be best if you were frank with me. I enquired why you were travelling alone. Let me repeat the question."

She gave him a glance from under her eye-lashes and said:

"It is a secret, but I have urgent and important des-

8

patches which must be carried to London immediately! An ordinary messenger or courier would be in-
tercepted on the road, but it is unlikely that anyone
would suspect me!"

"Very dramatic!" the Duke remarked dryly. "And
now perhaps you will tell me the truth!"

"You do not believe me?"

"No!"

There was a silence and then the girl said:

"I do not wish to tell you the truth, and there is
no reason why you should demand it!"

"I think there is every reason," the Duke replied.
"After all, you are enjoying the hospitality of my coach,
and quite frankly I do not wish to be involved in any
scandal."

"There is no likelihood of that!" the girl said quickly—almost too quickly.

"Are you sure?" the Duke asked. "Perhaps it would
be best if I turn the coach round. Your own carriage
can doubtless be repaired, and you can wait at *The
Grouse and Thistle* until it is completed."

The girl thought for a moment and then in a very
different tone asked:

"If I tell you the truth, will you promise to help
me?"

"I can make no such promise," the Duke answered,
"but, shall I say, I shall give you a sympathetic hearing."

"That is not enough!"

"I am not prepared to offer more!"

Again there was a silence and at last in a small
voice the girl said:

"I have . . . run away!"

"I guessed that," the Duke observed.

"Is it very obvious?"

"Ladies—even Scottish ladies—do not travel unaccompanied and do not beg lifts from strangers!"

The girl did not answer and the Duke went on:

"Well, are you running away from school?"

"No, of course not!" came the response. "I am eighteen and grown up! As a matter of fact I have never been to school!"

"Then you are running away from home?"

"Yes!"

"Why?"

As she hesitated the Duke said:

"I must insist upon knowing the truth, and it will be easier if you tell me of your own free will without my compelling you to do so. Suppose for a start I learn your name?"

"Jacobina."

The Duke raised his eye-brows.

"Then I gather from that you are a Jacobite?"

"Of course I am!" the girl agreed. "And so are all my Clan. My grandfather died in the Rebellion of '45."

"And now the Young Pretender—Charles Stuart—is dead too," the Duke said. "You can hardly fight for a King who no longer exists."

"His brother, James, is still alive!" the girl answered quickly, "and if you think we would acknowledge those German upstarts in London as our rightful Monarchs you are very much mistaken!"

The Duke smiled to himself.

He was well aware of how loyal many of the Scots were to their Stuart Kings and he could not help admiring their courage. The English had never been able to destroy their persistent and obstinate adoration of the man who they thought of as 'Bonnie Prince Charlie.'

"Well, Jacobina," he said, "go on with your story."

"I am called Jabina," she said. "Jacobina is too much of a mouthful, but that is what I was christened and I am proud of it!"

"I can quite believe that!" the Duke said, "but do you think those who christened you would be proud of you at this particular moment? I imagine they will be searching for you."

"They will not be able to find me," Jabina said firmly.

"Start from the beginning!" the Duke said with a note of command in his voice which those who served him would have instantly recognised.

"I do not wish to talk about it," Jabina protested.

"I am afraid I must insist upon knowing why you are running away," the Duke said. "Otherwise, and make no mistake about this, Jabina, I shall take you back to *The Grouse and Thistle.*"

She looked at him speculatively, her eyes wide in her small face.

"I believe you would do something just as beastly as that!" she said at length. "You are a Sassenach. I have always known one can never trust a Sassenach!"

"But you have trusted me!" the Duke answered. "You are in my coach and therefore for the moment I am responsible for you. From what are you running away?"

"From being . . . married!" Jabina said in a low voice.

"You are engaged?"

"Papa had intended to announce the engagement next week."

"Did you tell your father you do not wish to be married?"

"I told him . . . but he would not listen."

"Why not?"

"He likes the man he has chosen for me."

"And you do not?"

"I hate him!" Jabina said fiercely. "He is old, dull, staid, and disagreeable!"

"What do you think your father will do when he finds you have disappeared?" the Duke asked.

"He will come tearing after me with a thousand of the Clan brandishing their claymores!"

"A thousand?" the Duke queried. "Surely that is somewhat an exaggeration?"

"I may exaggerate," Jabina retorted, "but I am certain that Papa will pursue me and he will be very angry!"

"I am not surprised!" the Duke remarked. "But as

far as I am concerned, I have no intention of being involved in your matrimonial troubles. We should reach the next Posting-Inn before nightfall, and after that you must fend for yourself!"

"I never asked you to take me any further!" Jabina said. "It is near the Border and once in England I can get a stage-coach to London."

"What do you intend to do in London?" the Duke enquired.

"I am not going to stay there," Jabina answered almost scornfully. "I am on my way to France. Now that the war with Bonaparte is over I can stay with my Aunt, Mama's sister. She married a Frenchman and lives near Nice."

"Have you informed your Aunt of this decision?"

"No. But she will be glad to see me . . . I know she will. She loved Mama, but she and Papa never got on together."

"Your mother is dead?"

"She died six years ago. I know that she would never have allowed Papa to force me into marriage with a man whom I detest!"

"I understand most girls have no choice when it comes to marriage," the Duke said slowly. "I am sure, Jabina, that your father knows what is best for you."

"That is just the pompous sort of thing you would say," Jabina said scathingly. "You are exactly like Lord Dornach!"

"Lord Dornach?" the Duke enquired. "Is that the man you are to marry?"

"Do you know him?" Jabina asked.

"No," the Duke answered, "but it sounds a very good marriage, and that is what most young women require."

"It is not what I require," Jabina said crossly.

"Lord Dornach is well off?"

"He is very rich, I believe," Jabina answered, "but if he were hung from head to foot in diamonds, it would not make me like him any the more. I told you he is old and dull. I would not be surprised if he incarcerated me in one of the dungeons beneath his Castle and beat me to death!"

"The trouble with you," the Duke remarked, "is that you have too fertile an imagination."

"That is exactly what Papa says."

"What more does your father say?"

"He says I am impetuous, impulsive, unstable, and in need of a strong, guiding hand!" Jabina recited.

Her voice held a note of contempt.

"A very accurate description, I should imagine," the Duke remarked dryly.

Jabina tossed her head.

"How would you like to be married off to someone who was chosen in order to train you to become different from what you are at present? Besides, when Lord Dornach proposed to me, he never even said he loved me!"

"I imagine," the Duke said in an amused voice, "that you hardly encouraged him to express himself ardently!"

"I certainly did not!" Jabina flashed. "I said to him: 'I would rather wed a codfish than you, My Lord!' "

The Duke laughed—he could not help it.

"I am afraid, Jabina," he said after a moment, "that your idea of travelling to Nice by yourself is quite impossible. It is sad for you to have to marry a man you dislike; but perhaps, having given your father a fright by running away, you will find him more reasonable on your return."

"I am not going back!" Jabina cried. "I have already told you. I am not going back! Nothing could make me!"

"Then that is your business," the Duke replied. "At the next Posting-Inn our ways will part."

"You are just like Pontius Pilate," Jabina said scornfully. "You are washing your hands of a problem simply because you do not know what to do about it."

For a moment the Duke looked startled.

He was not in the habit of hearing anyone speak to him in such a manner.

"It is not my problem," he said almost in self-defence.

"Injustice, cruelty, and brutality is everyone's problem," Jabina contradicted. "If you were a chivalrous sort of young man like the hero in a novel you would be prepared to fight for me; to help me escape from the forces of evil. You might even carry me away on your charger to the safety of your Castle!"

"It sounds very much like a Frances Burney or Mrs. Radcliffe!" the Duke remarked. "But unfortunately my Castle, as you call it, is a very long distance away, and having once got you there, I should find it difficult to explain your presence."

He smiled and added:

"The Knights who rescued distressed maidens in the past never seemed to have any problem as to what to do with them!"

"That is true," Jabina agreed. "At the same time I am surprised that you should realise it!"

The Duke did not reply. He simply raised his eyebrows and after a moment she said impulsively:

"I am sorry if that sounded rude, but you are reading a very musty old book. I was watching you when you were not speaking to me, and certainly it did not look very exciting."

"It is a treatise on Mediaeval manuscripts."

"There!" Jabina exclaimed. "You see what I mean! It certainly would not lead me to think that you would know about Knights errant or maidens in distress."

"Perhaps my education has been neglected on that particular point," the Duke said. "All the same, Jabina, I have to think of how I can persuade you to return to your father."

"You need not waste your words or your breath. I will not turn back. I am going to my Aunt."

"Have you money for the journey?" the Duke asked.

She smiled at him and he noticed she had a dimple on the left side of her mouth.

"I am not as nit-witted as you think," she replied. "I have fifteen pounds in my purse which I took out of the housekeeping money when the House-keeper was not looking, and I have brought all my mother's jewellery with me. I have it pinned inside my gown so I cannot show it to you. But I know it is very valuable and when I got to London I will sell it, and then I shall have more than enough money to journey to Nice."

"But you cannot travel all the way alone," the Duke expostulated.

"Why not?" Jabina asked.

"You are too young, for one thing."

She waited, a little smile on her lips.

"Go on . . ." she prompted.

While he hesitated, searching for the right words, she added:

". . . and too pretty for another. You might as well say it. I know I am pretty. Everyone has told me so for years."

"Are you not being somewhat conceited?" the Duke asked.

"Not in the slightest!" Jabina replied. "My mother was very lovely and I am like her. She was half French and lived in Paris before she married my father."

"You do not look French to me," the Duke said.

"That is because, like everyone who is ignorant, you expect all French women to be dark," Jabina answered. "My mother had red hair like mine, and surely you know that Josephine, the wife of Napoleon Bonaparte, is red-haired?"

Jabina tossed her head again—it was a habit of hers.

"I expect I shall be a great success in Paris!"

The Duke sought for words.

He wondered how could he possible explain to this impulsive young creature why she could not travel to Paris alone, and the sort of success she might have would certainly not be in accordance with the manner in which she had been brought up.

Then he told himself it was none of his business.

He must not, and there was no possible obligation or excuse for his doing so, get himself involved in what might prove a very unsavoury scandal.

He did not know Lord Dornach, but he was obviously a nobleman. The fact that his fiancée had run away would itself cause a great deal of gossip without the added information that she had been assisted in her flight by the Duke of Warminster.

The Duke began to see a number of dangers ahead in which he could not possibly get embroiled.

He settled himself a little more firmly in the corner of his seat in the carriage.

"You are quite right, Jabina," he said aloud, "in saying that this is your business and I have no right to interfere. When we get to the next Posting-Inn we will go our separate ways. And I think it would be best if we had no knowledge of each other's true identity."

"I already know who you are," Jabina replied. "You are the Duke of Warminster. I heard your coachman telling the Inn-keeper so when you arrived. I must say, I thought it was a joke or a trick."

"A joke or a trick?" the Duke questioned.

"Well, Dukes do not usually drive about with only two coachmen on the box, no footmen and no out-riders."

"My second carriage is behind," the Duke said before he could prevent himself.

He had had no intention of explaining his behaviour to this impertinent chit.

"Well that accounts for it. Even so, I think it is a shabby way to travel. Can you not afford better?"

"Of course I can afford better," the Duke replied almost hotly, "but I do not wish to be ostentatious. I think out-riders, except on special occasions, are quite unnecessary."

"If I were a Duke," Jabina said, "I would always have out-riders, and my own horses would travel ahead of me so that I would certainly not have to rely on those to be found at a Posting-Inn."

"My horses do travel ahead of me in the South," the Duke answered, "but in actual fact I came North in my yacht and it seemed quite unnecessary to send my own horses such a long distance when they were only conveying my servants."

"You came in a yacht! How fascinating! Where is it?"

"In the harbour at Berwick," the Duke answered, "and I intend to sail home down the Coast and up the Thames to London."

"Now that I call very original!" Jabina approved. "You are not as stuffy as I thought you were."

"Stuffy!" the Duke exclaimed.

"Well you are a rather dull sort of Duke," she said frankly. "You are not fashionably dressed, for one thing. Your cravat is too low, the points of your collar are not above your chin, and your hair is not cut correctly."

The Duke, who had always rather prided himself on his sober attire, felt quite unnecessarily piqued.

"There is no point," he said coldly, "in indulging in personal criticism, but perhaps later, Jabina, you will be thankful that I am staid, stuffy, and dull. Otherwise you might at this moment be finding yourself in a lot of trouble."

"What sort of trouble?" Jabina asked with quickened interest.

The Duke glanced at her, intending to answer scathingly. Then he realised that the look in her eyes was very innocent.

She really did not understand, he thought, in what danger she might have been had she climbed into the carriage of some of the Bucks or Dandies who frequented the Clubs of St. James's. There were a number who undoubtedly would have thought a young unattached girl easy prey.

The Duke did not speak and after a moment Jabina said:

"Tell me."

"Your whole behaviour is preposterous!" the Duke said in a stern voice. "And let me assure you once again, Jabina, that you cannot travel to London alone or cross France unaccompanied. It is an impossible scheme. And what is more, I do not intend to allow you to attempt anything so reprehensible, so dangerous."

"How are you going to stop me?" Jabina asked defiantly.

"I am going to hand you over to the Sheriff in the first town we come to," the Duke replied. "I shall place you in his charge and he will return you to your father."

She gave a little cry.

"No! You cannot do that! How can you be so cruel? So treacherous?"

"I am being neither. I am being sensible and, as a matter of fact, I am thinking of your own interests."

"I do not believe you!" she said rudely. "You are only worrying in case you are involved."

"You are being very childish!" the Duke said, "but I assure you it is for your own good."

"I hate things that are for my own good! Like sago pudding, bread and butter, and hot milk!"

She spoke petulantly and then asked:

"Why could you not have been a gay, exciting young man who would have positively wanted to help me?"

"I am sorry, Jabina," the Duke said firmly. "I am, as it happens, very sympathetic, although you do not think so. But I do know a little bit more about the world than you do, and I assure you I should be criminally negligent if I allowed you to set off on this mad journey alone."

There was silence.

"Do you . . . really mean that you will . . . hand me over to the . . . Sheriff?" Jabina asked at last in a small voice.

"I mean it!" the Duke answered firmly, "and I promise you, Jabina, that one day you will thank me."

"He will take me back to Papa, and I will have to marry Lord Dornach, and I shall hate you for the rest of my life! Do you hear? I shall hate you! Hate you!"

"I am sorry about that," the Duke answered, "but there is nothing else I can do."

"I shall make a wax image and stick pins in you," Jabina said, "and I hope it makes you suffer all the fires of hell!"

The Duke did not answer and they drove for a little while without speaking.

At length Jabina said pleadingly:

"Please do not go to the Sheriff. If you leave me at the Inn I will find someone else to . . . assist me. I am always lucky and people are . . . kind to me."

The Duke thought there was a probability of people being far too kind and not in a way she would expect!

Aloud he said almost apologetically:

"I am sorry, Jabina. It has to be the Sheriff. If I left you alone and unprotected it would lie heavy on my conscience."

"You are a beast!" Jabina exclaimed dismally. "I had no idea anyone could be so horrible or so cruel. If I throw myself over a cliff rather than marry Lord Dornach, it will be all your fault, and that is something that will really be on your conscience for the rest of your life!"

The Duke did not answer and again they drove along in silence.

Now the wind had abated a little, but it was snowing hard. Soft snowflakes flopped against the windows and collecting there made it almost impossible to see out.

The road too seemed to have become rougher and the coach rocked precariously from side to side, but the horses still plodded on.

The Duke bent forward and rubbed at the window in an attempt to peer out to see where they were.

It was nearly dark now and he wondered apprehensively whether when darkness fell they would be able to find the Inn.

As if she read his thoughts Jabina said:

"Perhaps we shall be marooned in the snow and freeze to death and when we are found they will wonder who the strange girl is beside you."

She laughed.

"Think what a scandal that would be! 'The pompous Duke of Warminster found dead in the arms of a nameless Scottish beauty!' "

"As I told you once before," the Duke said, "you are far too conceited."

"Perhaps you do not admire red hair?"

"Not particularly!"

"I know exactly what sort of woman you like," Jabina taunted. "A quiet, mousy little creature who says, 'Yes, Your Grace' and, 'No, Your Grace!' She agrees with everything you say and never puts a foot out of place."

"At least she would not create a situation like this," the Duke replied.

"No, of course she would not," Jabina said sharply. "But think how deadly dull she would be to live with. It would be just like reading one of your musty old books over and over again."

She laughed lightly.

"There would be no surprises and it really would not matter if you go on to the next chapter or stay on the one you have just read, because there would never be anything new."

The Duke, with his eyes turned to the window, sighed.

"I assure you, Jabina, I have no desire for the adventures upon which you seem to thrive," he said. "All I am hoping is that we reach the Posting-Inn in safety."

"Worrying about it will not help," Jabina answered. "What you should get is a coachman on whom you can rely—or drive the horses yourself!"

"Higman has been with me for fifteen years . . ." the Duke began.

Suddenly he laughed.

"Really, Jabina, I believe you are trying to provoke me. I have never met such an irritating young woman in the whole of my life!"

"You are lucky!" Jabina said. "If your dull, musty sweetheart was with you now she would doubtless be in tears and clinging to you like a piece of frightened ivy!"

The Duke was about to reply when the coach gave

a sudden lurch and the wheels seemed to stick either in snow or mud.

It stopped at a somewhat precarious angle and the Duke opened the window nearest to him.

Instantly snowflakes came flooding in, blown by the wind which while it had abated was still quite strong.

The Duke put his head out the window.

"What is the matter, Higman?" he called. "Are we stuck?"

Even as his voice rang out the coach turned over. . . .

Chapter Two

The Duke opened his eyes and for a moment found it difficult to focus his sight.

He then saw two grey-green eyes beneath some tumbled red curls and with an effort remembered where he had seen them before.

"You are awake!" an ecstatic voice exclaimed. "I am so glad!"

A sudden weakness made the Duke close his eyes only to open them again quickly as he remembered the crash of the falling coach and the pain that had shot through his head before it brought oblivion.

"Where am I?" he asked, and was relieved to hear his own voice sounding almost normal.

"I have been so worried about you!" Jabina exclaimed. "I thought you would never wake up! In fact at first I thought you were dead!"

"The coach turned over," the Duke said, speaking slowly but distinctly. "Was anyone hurt?"

"Only you. You were looking out and your head must have struck a rock. The doctor has put six stitches in it!"

The Duke tried to raise his hand, but found that it was underneath the bed-clothes and was aware for the first time that he was in bed.

Under the circumstances, he told himself, he was surprisingly clear-headed. However his mouth was dry and he felt thirsty.

As if she read his thoughts, Jabina said:

"Would you like a drink? I have some lemonade here."

She poured out a glass and brought it to him. Putting her arm under his head in quite an expert fashion, she raised him so that he could drink.

As he drank he noticed with some detached part of his mind that the glass was of engraved crystal and that the sheets which covered him were of fine linen.

It hurt his head to move and when he had drunk a little of the lemonade he lay back against the pillows and thought it was almost too much trouble to go on asking questions.

Then he remembered Jabina was with him and made an effort.

"Is this an—Inn?" he asked, thinking as he spoke that the room seemed very large and impressive for what was usually obtainable in a road-side Posting House.

"No indeed," Jabina replied. "We are at the home of Sir Ewan and Lady McCairn. When the coach overturned one of their farm hands was passing and fetched assistance from the house."

'It sounds very satisfactory,' the Duke thought and fell asleep.

It must have been several hours later when he awakened to find that Jabina was still with him.

The lights were lit in the room and the curtains drawn over the windows.

Jabina was sitting by the fire-side and he watched her for a moment without her being aware of it, noticing the manner in which the firelight lit up the vivid red of her hair.

He saw too that her figure, silhouetted against the firelight, was very young and graceful.

He did not speak, but she must have been instinctively aware that he was awake, for she turned her head and he saw her eyes light up with pleasure when she saw him watching her.

She rose and came to the bed-side.

"Do you feel better?" she asked. "The Doctor has

24

been in and is very pleased with your wound. He says he is doubtful if it will even show after a year or so."

"A year or so?" the Duke repeated. "It is fortunate that I am not vain about my looks!"

"As a matter of fact," Jabina said frankly, "I was thinking that you looked quite handsome and interesting with a bandage round your head! You might easily be the hero of one of the romantic books I like reading."

"It is a part I have no wish to play!" the Duke said firmly. "And as soon as I am well enough, I must be on my way South."

"It will be at least three days before the Doctor allows you to get up," Jabina answered. "You are very lucky your injury was no worse!"

"Tell me exactly what happened!" the Duke commanded.

"It is rather difficult to remember in all the excitement," Jabina replied, "but apparently the wheels of the coach went into a ditch or a trough under the snow. When the carriage turned over it fortunately fell on so much snow that nothing was broken, not even the glass in the lamps!"

"And the horses?" the Duke asked.

"They were all right, only rather frightened. Your coachmen led them here and they are housed in the stables waiting for us to continue our journey."

The Duke raised his eye-brows.

"Us?" he enquired.

Jabina, who was standing by his bed, looked away from him.

There was something in her manner which told the Duke that she was uneasy and perhaps embarrassed.

"What is it?" he asked. "What has happened?"

"I think I will tell you tomorrow," Jabina said. "It is only that—"

She stopped.

"Only what?" the Duke enquired.

"I do not wish you to talk to anyone about . . . us until I have told you . . . something."

The Duke tried to raise himself a little against his

pillows but the effort hurt his head and instead he said:

"Come here, Jabina! Come near me! I want to look at you."

She hesitated as if she would refuse him, then she turned and came two steps nearer.

"Now," the Duke said, looking into her face, "tell me what you are trying to hide from me, for I am well aware there is something!"

"It really would be better for me to tell you when you are well."

"I am perfectly well now," the Duke replied. "I am not such a weakling that a blow on the head will knock me out permanently!"

"It was a very nasty cut," Jabina said. "You bled profusely! I thought you must be dead! I was terrified! I was . . . really!"

"I can well believe it," the Duke answered, "but I am still waiting to hear what you have to tell me, Jabina."

She would have moved away but he reached out his hand and held on to her wrist.

"Tell me!" he ordered. "I know that something is wrong and the sooner I learn about it, the better!"

He felt Jabina quiver and was surprised.

Then she said hesitatingly:

"It is . . . just that when we . . . arrived here at . . . the house, you were being carried on a gate that was lifted from its hinges, Lady McCairn . . . recognised me!"

The Duke was still.

This was something he had not expected.

"You mean—you have met her before?" he asked.

"Yes, some years ago," Jabina answered, "and she knows my father, although they dislike each other heartily."

"I see!" the Duke said slowly, "so it was rather difficult for you to explain why you were in my coach. Did you tell her you had run away from home?"

There was a silence.

"What did you tell her, Jabina?" the Duke asked, tightening his hold on the small wrist.

For a moment he thought Jabina was not going to answer and then the words seemed to burst from her lips.

"I told her we were ... married!"

"Married?"

The Duke was so astounded that he let Jabina's wrist go and, lying back against his pillows, could find no words with which to express himself.

"There was ... nothing else I ... could do," Jabina explained. "I had no time to ... think ... I was not expecting to see Lady McCairn ... and when she said to me: 'Jabina Kilcarthie! What are you doing here?' I just panicked."

"So you said we are married!" the Duke exclaimed.

"Well, Lady McCairn then asked: 'Who is this man?' and I replied: 'He is my husband!'"

The Duke digested this information for a moment and then he said:

"Well, the sooner I see Lady McCairn and explain the circumstances to her, the better!"

"You cannot do that!" Jabina cried. "You cannot! She has told everyone in the house that I am your wife. I have been given the room next door and she expects me to nurse you. It is the sort of thing a wife would do."

"My dear child," the Duke said, "there is only one possible way to extricate ourselves from this impossible coil in which you have involved us, and that is to tell the truth."

"And what do you suppose Lady McCairn will think then?" Jabina asked. "We were travelling together; going towards the Posting-Inn where we were both staying. She would hardly think it correct behaviour on your part ... let alone mine!"

There was some sense in this and the Duke digested it slowly.

Then suddenly he exclaimed angrily:

"Why the devil did you not tell the truth? How

could you be so foolish—so incredibly naive as to say that we were married?"

"As I told you, I did not have time to think," Jabina explained.

"But surely Lady McCairn will tell your father that we have been here?"

Jabina seated herself on the side of the bed.

"Well, I worked it out this way," she said seriously. "Lady McCairn dislikes my father and he loathes her. He says she is a malicious old gossip—which she is!"

"That of course is a great help!" the Duke remarked sarcastically.

"What I thought was," Jabina went on as if he had not spoken, "that if I had told her we were not married, she would have been delighted to write to Papa so as to make trouble and make him feel embarrassed because his daughter was behaving badly."

"Which you are!" the Duke remarked crossly.

"On the other hand," Jabina continued, ignoring his remarks, "as she thinks I am married to a Duke, she is so piqued that I have made such a good marriage that I doubt if she will mention it to anyone—let alone Papa!"

There was some sort of twisted logic in this, the Duke thought. At the same time he was appalled at the position in which Jabina had put him.

"We will go away as soon as you are better," Jabina went on soothingly. "When I have reached my Aunt in France and am living there, everyone will soon forget about me. After all, Scotland is a long way from your Estates in England."

"The whole thing is preposterous!" the Duke stormed. "I am sure that the sensible thing for me to do would be to tell Lady McCairn the truth. I will inform her that I was merely giving you a lift; that I had never even set eyes on you before yesterday."

"I am quite certain Lady McCairn will never believe that sort of story," Jabina retorted. "She would be certain that you were abducting me, or that there was some discreditable reason why we should be alone together late in the evening in a coach. She is the sort of person who always suspects the worst."

'How could any man,' the Duke asked himself, 'have got into such a fix merely by performing a kindly action and giving an elderly lady a lift?'

He felt like shaking Jabina, but it was at the moment too much of an effort even to be angry with her.

Perched on the side of his bed, her eyes watching him with an apprehensive expression in them, she looked, he had to admit, extremely attractive, which did not make the situation any better.

As he did not speak, Jabina said after a moment:

"You do see that explanations will only make things worse?"

"I do not believe anything could be worse!" the Duke replied gloomily. "You have certainly managed to damage my reputation, Jabina, and as for yours . . . !"

"Our reputations at the moment are as pure as the driven snow," Jabina contradicted, "and Lady McCairn is purring like a Cheshire Cat at the thought of having a Duke as her guest."

She smiled and the dimple appeared at the side of her mouth.

"I had no idea you were so important. I am really rather impressed with you now."

"I am glad to hear it!" the Duke said. "Perhaps you will now be a little more polite!"

"I still think that you are far too dull and staid," she said frankly. "When I think that you could be part of the Carlton House Set I cannot believe that you find those musty old books more interesting!"

"I thought you did not approve of the German upstarts who constitute our Monarchy!" the Duke remarked.

Jabina laughed.

"That is of course a score to you!" she exclaimed. "But at the same time the extravagances, the drinking, the gambling, the parties and Balls must all be very entertaining."

"Who has been telling you all this?" the Duke asked. "Lady McCairn?"

"She is an absolute fund of information about everything and everybody," Jabina replied. "She even knows the size of your Estates and how much money your father left you when he died."

The Duke groaned.

He was well aware that the gossiping busy-body would not hesitate to relate to all and sundry that she had entertained the Duke of Warminster and his Scottish bride.

"I suppose Lady McCairn enquired when we were married?"

Jabina blushed.

"I had to tell her something."

"Knowing that fertile imagination of yours," the Duke said, "I cannot believe you found it hard to invent a wedding, a honeymoon, and doubtless a prolonged courtship!"

Jabina was silent, and after a moment he said:

"The only solution is for us to get away from here as soon as possible and hope that Her Ladyship forgets our very existence."

"I am afraid she is not likely to do that," Jabina said. "At the same time I must escape from Scotland. I am so afraid that Papa will catch up with me."

"I can think of nothing that would please me more!" the Duke remarked.

Jabina hesitated a moment and then she asked slowly:

"You will not . . . hand me over to the . . . Sheriff?"

"I think at the moment that such an action would invite the very unpleasant publicity I am avowing to avoid."

"Oh, good!"

Jabina almost bounced on the bed.

"I thought you would change your mind after the accident. I looked after you . . . I did really. I might have run away and left you to die!"

"Unless both my servants had died in the accident as well, I cannot imagine that whether you stayed or went made much difference!"

"Oh, do stop being so dampening!" Jabina ejaculated. "After all, it was very frightening and if I had been that dull, musty sweetheart you are so keen on, I would just have sat down and cried!"

"What did you do as a matter of fact?" the Duke asked curiously.

"I crawled out of the coach," Jabina replied, "and helped the coachmen drag you free. We could see you were injured, and for a moment they did not know what to do. What with the horses plunging about and the wheels of the carriage waving in the air, it was a bit of a nightmare!"

She saw the Duke was listening and went on:

"I wiped some of the blood away from your forehead, and then I told your second coachman, who was not so concerned with the horses, to wave one of the carriage-lamps from side to side as a call for help. I shouted too, and as if by a miracle a farm-labourer appeared going home from work."

"So he told you where we were?"

"He said the house was quite near," Jabina answered. "It was not until too late that I learnt it was the home of Sir Ewan and Lady McCairn or I would have let you go there alone."

"I doubt it!" the duke said. "You were enjoying the drama. Tell the truth, Jabina!"

"Well, it was rather exciting," she admitted, "only I was so worried about you. It seemed there was only me to give orders. Your head coachman kept saying: 'His Grace would do this' and 'His Grace would do that.' But I said that as His Grace was not capable of speaking, I would give the orders. It was I who thought of carrying you on the gate."

"Why did they have to do that?" the Duke asked.

"The labourer came back with some men but they had not thought to bring with them anything on which they could carry you. They talked of going back for a carriage. But it was growing very cold by that time and you were lying in the snow."

She smiled.

"Of course I covered you with the rugs. I thought of that too!"

"I can see you were extremely resourceful," the Duke admitted, "and I suppose you are expecting me to be grateful to you?"

"I know you think I am a nit-wit," Jabina replied. "All I am trying to point out is that another woman . . . the sort of trembling creature you like . . . would have been quite useless in an emergency!"

She had spoken scornfully and she went on:

"On the other hand, the Scots are always ready to improvise and that is exactly what I did!"

"So I must thank you."

"You are not still . . . cross with me . . . are you?"

"I am furious!" the Duke replied, "but there is really nothing I can do about it at the moment."

"I thought you would see sense!" Jabina said frankly.

"Sense!" the Duke groaned. "There is nothing sensible about the whole situation, but as you have got us into this mess, I cannot for the life of me see any way out of it except flight!"

"That is exactly what I thought," Jabina agreed with satisfaction.

The following morning the Duke was visited by Lady McCairn.

She was, he thought, the type of domineering, gossip-loving woman that he most disliked, and in a way he could understand Jabina's action in saying they were married rather than telling her the truth.

Lady McCairn was, she assured the Duke, delighted to have been of assistance to him.

In the space of a few minutes she mouthed over the names of a number of distinguished personages with whom they were both acquainted, and by only the slightest inflection of her voice conveyed the impression that she was surprised in the Duke's choice of a bride.

When she had left the bed-chamber, admonishing Jabina to take good care of her husband and speed his recovery, Jabina made a grimace.

"You see what she is like?" she said to the Duke.

"I do indeed," he replied. "It only confirms my impression that nothing could be more unfortunate than that we have to acccept her hospitality."

"If only the coach had turned over near a Posting-Inn, none of this would have happened," Jabina said regretfully.

"I see no reason why it should have turned over at all," the Duke replied. "Higman is a very experienced driver, but of course on roads such as Scotland provides for travellers there is no knowing what might happen!"

"Scottish roads are perfectly all right at most times of the year!" Jabina retorted. "But if Sassenachs are so foolish as to travel during the winter when there is snow and gales, they must put up with what they get!"

"That is exactly what I am trying to do!" the Duke said patiently, "but I had not anticipated having anyone like you as an encumbrance round my neck!"

"Well, I have decided to leave you as soon as we are across the border," Jabina said proudly. "I can assure you I have no desire to stay where I am not wanted!"

The Duke laughed.

When she was annoyed, Jabina looked like a small kitten which had been affronted, and lying in bed with no-one else to talk to he was finding it increasingly hard to be as angry with her as he wished to be.

He found her exasperating, but at the same time he could not help being amused by many of the things she told him.

He realised that her father's description of her was very accurate. She was undoubtedly impetuous and impulsive, but at the same time she had a warm heart and an amusing wit, which sometimes made him chuckle in the depths of the night when she had left him for her own room.

"Be careful what you say in front of the servants," she admonished the Duke. "They have been talking to your coachmen, and of course it was a surprise to your own staff that we are supposed to be married."

"Have the maids questioned you about it?" the Duke asked.

"Not exactly," Jabina replied, "but I guessed what had happened. I told them it was a dead secret that we had been married because you had not yet broken the news to your aged relatives, who must learn about it before anyone else."

"I can see the plot thickens and thickens," the Duke said gloomily. "Of course Higman and Clements must have been astonished to learn that you were passing yourself off as the Duchess of Warminster when they knew quite well we had met only the day before."

He could see that a number of explanations would have to be made even to his own servants, and on the day before the Doctor had said he could do so he made his plans to depart.

Looking rather pale but, as Jabina told him, interesting, he went down to dinner the night before with a bandage round his head and managed adroitly to parry a number of embarrassing questions which Lady Mc-Cairn had not unexpectedly prepared for him.

Fortunately Sir Ewan was only concerned with talking sport, and by retiring early to bed because of the journey that lay ahead of them the next day, the Duke managed to avoid too long an inquisition by his Hostess.

When they reached their own rooms Jabina shut the door behind them and said in a conspiratorial whisper:

"She was suspicious! I knew that whatever I said to the maids they were bound to tell her that the coachmen said we were not married. She asked me at least a dozen times in what Kirk the ceremony took place and whether my father was present. I have a feeling that she now thinks we have eloped!"

"Let her think so," the Duke said savagely. "I find the whole situation insupportable. We will leave to-morrow, and when we get away we will somehow concoct some sort of story for the rest of the world."

He paused and added:

"Anyway I cannot credit that anyone with any sense would believe what Lady McCairn says."

"People listen to what they want to hear," Jabina said, "and everyone enjoys scandal. You know that as well as I do!"

The Duke knew this was only too true but he was not prepared to enter into another discussion at this moment.

"Go to bed, Jabina!" he said sharply. "You need your beauty-sleep and I have given orders that we shall start off at nine o'clock precisely."

"You must not do too much the first day," Jabina warned. "As a matter of fact I have talked to Higman, and he says if we stay one night on the road we should reach Berwick about noon the following day, and he thinks that is a good time for you to embark on your yacht."

"Damnit all—will you let me make my own plans?" the Duke asked.

"I am still your nurse and ostensibly your wife until I leave you," Jabina replied with dignity, "and if you talked to either of those persons in such a rude manner they would be extremely surprised."

She spoke with such an offended dignity that the Duke found himself apologising.

"I am sorry, Jabina," he said. "It is only that Lady McCairn gets under my skin. The whole situation worries me. I am not usually so short-tempered."

"I forgive you!" Jabina replied generously. "Good-night, Your Grace."

She swept him a very elegant curtsy, and then with her eyes laughing up at him she added:

"You are quite certain you would not like me to come in later and smooth your pillow?"

"Go to bed!" the Duke said firmly, pushing her

through the communicating door and locking it behind her.

He had been aware all during dinner what a precarious position they both were in.

He could well imagine what Jabina's father's reaction would be to the news that his daughter was travelling through Scotland in the company of a Duke to whom she said she was married.

He also knew that if any of his friends got to hear of the position in which he found himself they would think it a tremendous jest.

His quiet scholarly life had not passed un-noticed. Nor could he avoid having his leg pulled on innumerable occasions by his contemporaries.

"Come and enjoy yourself in London, Drue," Freddie, one of his close friends with whom he had been at Oxford, begged him not once but a dozen times. "You will turn into a turnip-head if you stay in the country much longer."

Freddie also painted a vivid picture of the gaieties awaiting the Duke.

"The Prince of Wales will welcome you with open arms," he declared. "His Royal Highness likes his Dukes around him! And the pretty 'Cyprians' adore them!"

He laughed at the Duke's books and added:

"There are some new 'Venus's' from the Continent who will soon sweep away the dust accumulating over your eyes from too much reading!"

But the Duke refused all appeals to join the Gay Set which, as Jabina had rightly said, circled round Carlton House and the Prince of Wales, and showed no interest in 'Fashionable Impures.'

He had his own reasons for his dislike of the Social world, but while he was not prepared to divulge them, they hardened his determination to do as he wished, which was to live quietly in the country.

What Jabina had said jeeringly the day before about a musty sweetheart had however a ring of truth in it.

He had formed a liaison some years previously with

the young widow of a Librarian with whom he had become acquainted in the course of his studies. He had been an erudite man with whom the Duke had entered into a long correspondence.

Marguerite Blachett was a quiet, attractive, well-educated woman, some two years older than the Duke, with a soft, gentle, unassuming manner which had pleased him from the first moment he set eyes on her.

On her husband's death the Duke had called to offer his condolences and found that she was nearly as knowledgeable on the subjects in which he was interested as her husband had been.

They had entered into a correspondence, and then as she lived only seven miles from the Duke's Ancestral Home, he had found it increasingly convenient to call on her.

It had been a quiet, almost passionless affair, and the urgency of a physical contact had been more on her side than on his. He liked her and he found it a relief to be able to talk to someone about the literature he enjoyed.

Lying in the bed, the Duke could not help thinking how very different in every way Marguerite was from Jabina.

His mistress, if that was not an exaggerated term for someone with whom he found an easy companionship, seldom spoke without thinking.

He had never known her to be impulsive. He had never in fact known her to do anything that was unexpected or in any way reprehensible.

She would, he knew, disapprove of Jabina and find her quick impulsive nature so foreign to her own that the two women would certainly have nothing in common.

And as to Jabina's opinion of Marguerite, the Duke knew only too well what that would be!

He hoped that Marguerite would not hear of his adventures in Scotland, for she would undoubtedly be hurt by the idea that he might have married without telling her first.

He wondered how he would ever be able to explain to her, let alone his other friends, that marriage was indeed very far from his thoughts and he had no intention of tying himself to any woman at any time.

It was strange that a young man could have made up his mind so firmly and irrevocably that he would never marry.

Again the Duke had his reasons for this, although he had never confided them to anyone.

He was, he told himself, perfectly content and did not feel lonely in his enormous mansion. He did not crave to see a wife sitting at the opposite end of his table.

He was quite unperturbed by the fact that he would not have a son to inherit his Title and Estates.

He intended to remain a bachelor. He had chosen his way of life and, he told himself, it suited him very well. Everything about him was well-ordered.

In short, unless the roof collapsed over his head, which was very unlikely as he had it inspected at regular intervals, the chance of his being surprised by anything at Warminster House was, in racing terms, about a hundred to one against!

And yet, the Duke asked himself, how could he possibly anticipate that on quite an ordinary journey to Scotland this incredible situation should have arisen?

What he had to do was to find a way out of this dilemma and as quickly as possible. That, he told himself, was not as difficult as it seemed.

He would take Jabina, as she had requested, to the Border. After that he would leave her quite firmly to fend for herself.

He remembered thinking before the accident that it would be on his conscience to let a young, innocent girl journey to London alone and cross the Channel to France.

Perhaps he should find her a chaperone?

Then his thoughts shied away at the idea. Once again he would be embroiling himself.

If he engaged a chaperone, an elderly and respectable woman who would escort Jabina in a proper manner, then there would be explanations to be made and he would also have to explain to Jabina why such a person was necessary.

He felt as though everything encroached on his own privacy and self-sufficiency which was the way of life that he had chosen.

"It is not my business!" he said again.

Yet he wondered why the thought of Jabina setting off alone to France with her mother's jewellery pinned inside her gown should seem so poignant.

'Young women today are quite capable of looking after themselves,' he thought.

Then he found himself remembering the innocence in Jabina's eyes and the dimple that appeared at the corner of her mouth when she smiled.

The Duke turned over restlessly in his bed.

"Stop thinking about the girl!" he admonished himself. "She has already got you into enough trouble as it is! Do exactly as she has asked of you. Set her on the right road for London and go home by sea."

It was good advice and he told himself that he would follow it, however tiresome Jabina might be or however uncomfortably his conscience pricked him.

"I should have turned back and left her at *The Grouse and Thistle*," the Duke muttered.

Why on earth had he allowed himself to be beguiled into carrying her further?

As he asked the question the Duke found the answer in the fact that he knew few young women.

It seemed absurd, but going over his acquaintances he found it hard to remember when he had ever talked alone with a girl or entertained one at Warminster.

His House-parties, and there were not many of them, usually consisted of men of his own age who were unmarried.

When occasionally his relatives came to stay and he was forced to invite friends to meet them, they were nearly always couples older than himself.

"You are in a groove, Drue. It is time you got out of it," he could hear Freddie cry. "Come to London

and meet the 'Incomparables' who grace the Social
Balls and the 'Fashionable Impures' who adorn the
Nightclubs."

"I prefer being here," the Duke had averred.

"It is unnatural! You will become a pompous bore
before you are thirty!" Freddie had answered.

The Duke had merely laughed at him, but now, remembering that Jabina had called him old and stuffy,
pompous and dull, he wondered if in fact both she and
Freddie were speaking the truth.

"I am what I want to be," he said obstinately, but
found he said it with less conviction than he had done
in the past.

Again he turned over restlessly in bed.

He wanted to sleep and was well aware that he
would need all his strength tomorrow if he was to be
jolted about on the rough roads.

He had the idea that next door Jabina would be sleeping peacefully.

He was convinced that in her sleep she would look
very young and very innocent.

Then he told himself savagely it was not of the least
interest to him what she looked like!

The Duke, Sir Ewan, and Lady McCairn had finished
breakfast before Jabina appeared.

She rushed into the room like a small whirlwind,
curtsied to her Hostess, and was full of apologies.

"I meant to get up very early, and then I over-slept,"
she explained. "I went to sleep again after I was called.
Can you imagine anything more infuriating?"

"You should have asked your husband to awaken
you," Lady McCairn said. "I assure you it would be
very difficult for me to sleep once Sir Ewan decided to
get up!"

She spoke in a somewhat arch manner which told
the Duke all too clearly that she was trying to ascertain
if he and Jabina had slept in the same bed the night
before.

Jabina was quite unconscious of her Hostess's curiosity.

"I find it hard to get up in the morning," she confessed, "but I never want to go to bed!"

"From what I hear, His Grace does not keep late hours at Warminster," Lady McCairn said. "In fact, unlike the wild and most reprehensible behaviour of Social London, I am told Your Grace has chosen a more disciplined existence."

"That is true!" the Duke said briefly. "And now if you will excuse me, Ma'am, I will see that everything is in readiness for our departure."

He went from the Dining-Room and Lady McCairn turned to Jabina.

"You could not have made a wiser choice, my dear. You will enjoy a quiet, exemplary life at Warminster and the Duke will, I am sure, be a most commendable and reliable husband."

"Perhaps he is not as dull as he appears," Jabina said without thinking, and saw the astonishment on Lady McCairn's face.

"I am sure, dear Child, you do not mean what you say?"

There was a glint in Lady McCairn's eye as she spoke that made Jabina sure that this morsel of gossip would be repeated to everyone with whom she came in contact.

'She will think I married him only for his Title!' Jabina told herself, but she could not un-say what she had said.

She finished her breakfast quickly, well aware she should have kept a tighter bridle on her tongue.

She left the Dining-Room and at the top of the stairs which led to the front door found the Duke waiting for her.

As in most Scottish houses, the main rooms were on the first floor, and the wide stone staircase enabled them to walk down three abreast while Sir Ewan followed behind.

"I have not had a chance, Ma'am," the Duke said

pleasantly, "to tell you how charming I find your house. I can see some interesting examples of family portraits on your walls."

"We are very proud of our family collection," Lady McCairn replied. "This is the Chieftain who fought the Danes."

She pointed with a bony finger at a badly executed painting sorely in need of cleaning.

"A magnificent man!" the Duke commented.

"And here is the first Baronet, created of course after our James VI became also James I of England. And this is his wife, a pretty creature who produced no less than fourteen children, ten of whom survived!"

"Very commendable!" the Duke murmured.

They proceeded down some more stairs and then Lady McCairn said:

"This is our most romantic ancestor and her husband."

"Why romantic?" Jabina asked, interested by the adjective.

"In the Rebellion of '45, the McCairn Chieftain in the portrait had come to terms with the English who had granted him and his Clan immunity."

"And the lady?" Jabina asked with interest.

"Jean Ross was a neighbour who was found by the English to be spying on their troops. She was brought here to the Castle and condemned to death!"

"What happened?" Jabina asked, her eyes alight.

"She was just being taken away from the Great Hall in which the trial had taken place when Sir Angus McCairn, the Chieftain, who had become instantaneously infatuated with her beauty, spoke out."

"What did he say?" Jabina enquired excitedly.

"He said: 'You cannot kill this woman—she is my wife!' "

"And did that save her?" Jabina asked.

"But of course," Lady McCairn answered. "The English had granted Sir Angus and his Clan immunity."

"But they did not find out that there had been no marriage?"

Lady McCairn laughed.

"Surely, Jabina, you know our laws better than that? Marriage by Declaration in front of witnesses is completely legal in Scotland and the moment that Sir Angus spoke he and the lovely Jean were in truth man and wife!"

There was a moment's silence and Jabina was conscious that the Duke was standing still as if turned to stone.

"I am sure Your Grace knows of our Scottish customs," Lady McCairn chattered on. "For instance, if you and Jabina had not been married before you stayed with us, you are now legally and irrevocably man and wife."

There was a glint of malice in Lady McCairn's eyes as if she half-suspected the truth.

Neither Jabina nor the Duke spoke until they reached the front door.

"Good-bye, Jabina," Lady McCairn said. "It has been delightful having you and your husband here, and I hope that whenever you are visiting Scotland again we may offer you our hospitality."

"You are very kind," Jabina murmured.

The Duke shook hands with Sir Ewan and then with Lady McCairn. He too expressed his thanks and they climbed into the carriage.

They were covered with fur rugs and the foot-warmers were hot beneath their feet.

Higman flicked the horses with his whip and they set off down the long drive.

The Duke did not speak.

Jabina glanced at him from under her eye-lashes.

His chin was set square. His lips were pressed together in a tight line. He looked very stern and very angry.

After some moments, as if she could no longer bear the silence, she said in a very small voice hardly above a whisper:

"I am . . . sorry."

Chapter Three

The Duke did not answer.

He was in fact fighting for control of his temper.

Never in the whole of his life had he felt more like hitting somebody or swearing profanely.

He could hardly believe it was true that he, who had firmly made up his mind not to marry, should suddenly find himself in the position of being married to a girl of whom he had little knowledge and whom he found extremely irritating.

A surge of impotent fury made everything round him seem red, and he had an almost irresistible impulse to take Jabina by the shoulders and shake her until her teeth rattled.

Then the cold, logical part of his brain that had always controlled all he did told him that this would achieve nothing

What had happened could for the moment at any rate not be changed, and although he felt there must be a legal loop-hole somewhere, he could think of nothing save the fact that his wife—the Duchess of Warminster—was seated beside him.

He looked so fierce and so grim in his rage that Jabina was awed into silence.

She was not used to people who were emotional.

Her father was a dour man, who since her mother's death had communicated little with her save in monosyllables.

Anyone else might have been cast into despondence by the life she had led but in fact Jabina's natural buoyancy and vivid imagination had helped her to survive what had undoubtedly at the time been a depressing loneliness.

Her father's house was set in the midst of his Estate, with a three-mile drive to the nearest village.

With only aged servants to talk to, some of whom had been there in the time of her grandfather, Jabina was starved of companionship and had found some compensation by peopling her world with her own fantasies.

Because she craved excitement she made everything an adventure.

The first wild primrose of Spring was a moment for wild elation. A strong wind blowing across the moors became in her mind a typhoon which might take the roof off the house and leave them open to the elements and shivering in their beds.

When she went riding, she would imagine herself to be one of her ancestors riding into battle against the English, or at other times as she turned for home she was a Chieftain's daughter fleeing from the Vikings who would abduct her and carry her across the sea as their prisoner.

When she was not studying, for her father insisted on her having a good education, she was reading, and naturally the books which excited her most were romances of all sorts.

She identified herself with the heroines and lived through every adventure, sighed every sigh, wept every tear. And if, as so often happened in the books, the heroine died of a broken heart, Jabina herself felt that her life was finished.

It was a vicarious existence and, had he known of it, it would have explained to the Duke her habitual exaggerations and her love of the dramatic.

But nothing she had experienced through the lives of her heroines in fiction or history had prepared Jabina for sitting closely in a jolting carriage with a man who was obviously incensed to the point of violence and who showed a white line of fury above his pressed lips.

She wanted to try to explain that she had of course completely forgotten that Marriage by Declaration was a lawful way of being wed in Scotland.

She had heard about it; read about it. But when she had said in answer to Lady McCairn's question that the Duke was her husband, she had not for one second intended it to be anything but a quick falsehood.

A lie by which she could gain time to extricate herself from the uncomfortable predicament of being found alone in a damaged coach with a young man.

The only experience Jabina had had of men, or indeed of Society, had been the previous year when three months after her seventeenth birthday her father had taken her to Edinburgh for the Season.

There, as a débutante, she had been invited to Balls and Assemblies and had discovered that she could both attract and entertain men.

The younger men who attended such Social gatherings were not particularly outstanding. In fact to Jabina they seemed rather gauche, unpolished, and without many brains.

But there had been older men who, because she was animated and gay and stood out even amongst girls who were more classically beautiful, had flattered her and convinced her that to them she was very alluring.

Jabina had been strictly chaperoned. Her father had seen to that!

Nevertheless when she returned home it was with a new self-confidence and a feeling that outside the full, rather dismal world in which she lived there was another, exciting, exhilarating, and desirable.

She had also learnt during her visit to Edinburgh how to handle her father a little better than she had done in the past.

She realised that a man could be coaxed, flattered, and beguiled into doing what a woman wanted him to do, and she had managed to persuade her father that it was his duty to take her to Edinburgh again this May.

Then like a bombshell came the proposal from Lord Dornach!

Jabina had hardly noticed His Lordship. He was a friend of her father's, a frequent visitor to the Estate for the shooting, and who dropped in when he was passing the house on his way to Edinburgh or visiting other friends in the vicinity.

She thought him dull and almost as dour as her father.

His Lordship had a habit of pausing before he spoke which Jabina found annoying, because she was never quite certain, having asked him a question, whether he had heard it or was pondering on what should be his reply.

She had always thought of him as her father's friend, and when one day Sir Bruce told her to come to his study after Lord Dornach had left the house she had obeyed blithely, having no idea what was in store.

"I have something of great importance to tell you, Jabina," her father began, having cleared his throat.

"Yes, Papa. What is it?"

"Lord Dornach has offered for your hand in marriage and I have accepted on your behalf."

For a moment Jabina thought she could not have heard aright, that her father must be making some obscure joke. Then, as the full force of what he had said penetrated her brain, she gave a little cry of sheer horror.

"Marry Lord Dornach, Papa? I would not think of it!"

"I do not intend to argue on this matter, Jabina," her father replied. "I have given it my serious consideration and I think that His Lordship is exactly the right husband for you. I shall be glad to know that you will be in safe hands."

"But he is old, Papa . . . far too old to marry someone of my age!"

"That is a matter of opinion," her father replied. "You are inclined to be flighty, Jabina, and as I have told you before you are far too impetuous and impulsive. You need an older man to protect you."

"I do not want protecting!" Jabina almost shouted. "I want to marry someone I love! Someone with whom I can have fun."

"There is nothing more to be said, Jabina," Sir Bruce had said coldly. "Lord Dornach will call tomorrow, and you will receive him pleasantly and confirm my agreement that you should be his wife!"

"I will not! I will not marry him!" Jabina cried, stamping her foot.

"Do not speak to me in such a manner," Sir Bruce said icily. "Go to your room, Jabina, and stay there until you are in a better frame of mind. You are an extremely fortunate young woman and there is no more to be said on the matter."

"I will not do it, Papa!" Jabina said through gritted teeth.

"You will do as you are told!" Sir Bruce answered. "I am your father and you will obey me. I have nothing more to say to you on the subject."

He walked from the room closing the door behind him and Jabina had sunk down trembling on the hearthrug in front of the fire.

She was afraid of her father. She always had been. He had always seemed unapproachable, and even more so since the death of her mother.

But even her mother had never been able to sway him once he had made up his mind.

Jabina knew by the inflexion in his voice and the determination in his expression that, battle though she might, she would finally walk up the aisle and marry Lord Dornach.

She put her hands up to her face despairingly.

How could she bear it? How could she tolerate not only the man, whom she positively disliked, but the life she would lead as his wife?

She knew Dornach Castle. A gaunt, stone edifice, cold and drear, with thick walls three feet in width and dark, cheerless rooms which seemed somehow like the dungeons which lay beneath the Castle itself.

She thought of Lord Dornach touching her and felt herself shiver with a fear she had never known before.

He was as dark and frightening as his Castle.

She had a feeling that once incarcerated there she would scream with fear and no-one would hear her.

'I cannot marry him . . . I cannot!' she whispered to herself.

Yet the following day when Lord Dornach came to visit her she could not defy him as she wished to do.

It was only in her thoughts that she said the words that she told the Duke she had spoken aloud.

In actual fact with her father present she had stood with downcast eyes while Lord Dornach had slipped a heavy diamond ring on her finger.

It had belonged to his mother, and Jabina could not help noticing that it needed cleaning, while the setting was heavy and rather ugly.

"I feel sure we shall be very happy," Lord Dornach said ponderously after some thought.

"My daughter is shy," Sir Bruce said when Jabina did not answer. "It is not surprising, considering the honour that Your Lordship has accorded her."

Lord Dornach had looked down at Jabina's white face and for a moment she thought of appealing to him to let her go, not to want her as his wife.

Then some new instinct which she had lately developed where men were concerned told her that he did really desire her in that capacity.

It was nothing he said.

It was just that there was some flicker at the back of his eyes which was more frightening than if he had taken her in his arms.

She knew then that while she had never noticed him particularly, he had certainly noticed her.

She could not mistake the feeling she had about him.

It was the same as her reaction in Edinburgh when men clasped her hand too long or came too near when they were talking, and which she had sensed lay behind the flattering things they said to her.

Then it had been an excitement to know that she could arouse an emotion she did not quite understand, but was aware that it was a masculine response to her femininity.

What had been exciting and amusing in a young man was to Jabina revolting in a man old enough to be her father.

She had a wild impulse to turn and run away from him.

Only when she was at last alone and her father had taken Lord Dornach away to look at the horses in the stables had she known what she must do.

It had taken her some time to put her plan into action.

First she had thought she might simply leave the house and journey to Edinburgh to find one of the friends she had made the previous Season and ask if she could stay with her.

But she realised that her father would simply fetch her back and the situation would not change.

She would merely be more closely guarded and confined until the day she walked into the Kirk to become the wife of Lord Dornach.

It was then she remembered her Aunt, her mother's sister whom she had loved as a child.

Jabina had only to think of something to glamourise it and want to do it immediately!

To think of her Aunt living in Nice was to conjure up a haven of security in which it would be impossible for her father to find her.

She had a feeling, although she could not be certain, that he did not know her Aunt's address.

She had certainly never communicated with him since her sister's death, but she used to write to Jabina on her birthday and at Christmas.

Sometimes too when war did not prohibit it, presents arrived from France which was to Jabina a very special and thrilling treat.

There had been a pair of thin suede gloves with pearl buttons; fashioned by nuns were night-gowns of finest muslin, inset with lace and made with such perfect tiny stitches they might have been the work of fairy creatures.

There had been lace-edged handkerchiefs and other gifts all in exquisite taste, which were just the type of personal adornment to please a growing girl.

'Aunt Elspeth will understand,' she told herself, 'that I cannot marry a man like Lord Dornach, however rich and important he may be!'

She had a feeling that if she once reached her Aunt she would be able to find in the South of France the young man of her dreams.

He was handsome and laughing. A man with a twinkle in his eye, who would tell her not only of his admiration but also of his love.

She wanted to hear someone speak of all the things that had never been spoken of in her home. She wanted to be flattered; to feel not once but a thousand times the strange, breathless excitement in her throat when a man said:

"You are very lovely!"

But now she was married to a man who had made it quite obvious he detested her.

Jabina could hardly bear to think of it.

For a moment she contemplated screaming aloud that she had not meant this to happen and she could not endure the thought of the future.

The Duke was not at all the type of young man who had featured in her dreams.

When she thought of his stiff, unbending manner, the way in which he had disapproved of her exaggerations, of her boasting, and most of all of her running away from home, she felt that Fate had played her a dirty trick.

She had escaped from Lord Dornach only to marry what seemed to her at the moment to be no better than a younger version of him.

"What can I do? What can I do?"

It seemed to Jabina that the wheels as they rolled over the rough roads were repeating the words over and over again.

Then she had an idea.

"Do you think . . . ?" she began aloud.

The Duke turned to look at her for the first time.

Almost instinctively Jabina shrank back to the corner of the carriage.

His face was contorted with anger. This was not the phlegmatic, quiet man whom she had found rather boring and pompous ever since they had first met.

This was a man angry to the point of violence, his eyes flashing at her, and his voice harsh and bitter as he said aloud:

"You will be silent! We will discuss this when I have had time to think about it. For the moment I do not wish to hear your chattering voice and foolish comments!"

He turned his face from her to stare straight ahead, and for once Jabina was abashed into silence.

They drove on without speaking until at noon they drew into the yard of a Posting-Inn.

The Duke alighted and requested a private parlour, only to be told there was none available, and if they wished a meal they must take it in the communal Dining-Room where there were already a number of guests.

To Jabina it was a relief that she did not have to sit alone with him in silence or, alternatively, hear him rage at her.

With a quick swing of her emotional temperament after having been cast into dark despondency at the Duke's anger, now her spirits rose a little, especially as she realised she was hungry.

As usual the menu consisted of Scotch broth, tough mutton, and a suet pudding that was as heavy as lead!

But there was some excellent cheese and Jabina, with the healthy appetite of the young, ate heartily.

She noticed that the Duke only picked at his food

and drank with a wry expression on his face the inferior wine which was the best the Inn could provide.

She had the feeling, and rightly, that his head was hurting him and that he had found the jolting of the carriage extremely uncomfortable.

But he had told her not to speak, and with a great effort she bit back the words as they came to her lips and managed to remain silent.

Instead she contented herself with watching the people in the room and, as was her wont, making up stories about them. She could not help wondering what they thought about her.

She and the Duke certainly looked out of place amongst the roughly dressed sheep-farmers and slick, commercial travellers who accounted for the majority of the Inn's other clients.

Within an hour of their arrival they set off once again and now there was no doubt that the Duke was suffering.

He leant back in the corner of the carriage and closed his eyes, but even in repose he still looked angry.

Jabina, after glancing at him apprehensively, decided to keep the silence he had demanded of her.

On and on they went for what seemed an unending period of time until finally, just when the sun was sinking, they drew up at a Posting-House which even at a glance looked superior to the others at which they had called.

The Inn-keeper's wife, a woman of perhaps fifty, sensed they were Quality as soon as they appeared and ushered them into a private parlour where a huge log fire was burning in the grate and there were comfortable arm-chairs facing the hearth.

"Y'll be awanting two chambers, Sir, I gather, for ye and ye sister," the woman said to the Duke, having taken a quick glance at Jabina's left hand and seeing no ring.

"Yes, yes! That is exactly what we require," the Duke replied quickly.

"There be two on the first floor that'll suit ye admirably," the woman said. "If ye'll come with me, Miss, I'm sure ye would like to wash and tidy up afore supper, which'll be served immediat."

Knowing that countryfolk dined at five o'clock, Jabina meekly followed the Inn-keeper's wife upstairs to find two pleasant, low-ceilinged rooms with comfortable beds and chimney-pieces where fires were quickly kindled.

Hot water was brought, and after Jabina had washed and changed her gown she went somewhat hesitatingly down the polished oak stairs to the parlour.

She noticed that the Duke had changed his cravat and his travelling clothes and now wore another of the plain dark coats which she found reminiscent of a Minister rather than of a Gentleman of Fashion.

He was drinking a glass of brandy when she appeared and rose perfunctorily to his feet only to sit down again as she drew nearer to the fire, holding out her small hands to the blaze.

"The Inn-keeper's wife," he said at length, "thought you were my sister, and I think in the circumstances it would be wise to let such an impression stand. The servants unfortunately have already told her my name so it would be best for her to think for the short time we are here that that is our relationship."

Jabina had no chance of saying anything in reply, for at that moment the door was opened and the supper was brought in.

It was surprisingly good.

Instead of the tough mutton which was usually served at Posting-Inns, there was a tender sirloin of beef, fat pigeons stuffed with mushrooms, an un-cut ham, and brawn of which the Duke had a second helping.

There was also a choice of sweet-meats and puddings, followed by three cheeses, the best one being made from goat's milk.

The Landlord produced from his cellar a bottle of claret which the Duke found quite palatable, and by the end of the supper Jabina felt he must be in a more pleasant mood.

She was however not certain; for there was still a frown between his eyes as he looked at her, and while his face was no longer contorted with rage, she thought there was an ominous squareness about his chin and a firmness about his mouth which still made her feel apprehensive.

When at last the supper was finished and the table cleared, the Duke rose to sit at the fire-side with a glass of wine in his hand.

Somewhat nervously Jabina took the chair opposite him.

"And now," he said with a sharp note in his voice, "I suppose we shall have to discuss this intolerable situation in which we find ourselves."

"I . . . I am . . . sorry," Jabina said again.

"I must admit to finding it almost incomprehensible," the Duke said, "that you should have overlooked such an obvious outcome of your lies once you had made them."

He was still extremely incensed, Jabina thought with a sinking of her heart.

"I had . . . forgotten about the . . . law."

"You knew about it?" the Duke asked.

"Y-yes," Jabina answered, "but I have never actually known anyone who was Married by Declaration, and when I told Lady McCairn we were married, I just said it without . . . thinking."

"With disastrous results!"

"It must be . . . possible to free . . . ourselves of each other," Jabina murmured.

"Perhaps there is another law which makes that possible," the Duke suggested, "or is that also something you have forgotten?"

"I cannot think now why I said it," Jabina said almost pleadingly. "It was just that when I saw her looking at me with those beady eyes, I could not think of any other explanation of our being together and it just . . . came to my lips."

"You are quite certain you did not do it deliberately?" the Duke enquired.

For a moment Jabina did not understand what he was saying. Then a flush rose in her cheeks.

"Do you really think," she retorted with some spirit, "that I wanted to be married to you? Even if you are a Duke, you are not at all the sort of man I wish to marry. You are far too dull and disagreeable! And, if it comes to that, far too old!"

She thought the Duke looked at her with contempt and was stung into saying rudely:

"It is no use being a Duke if you are just a stick-in-the-mud! I cannot imagine any girl wanting you as her husband!"

"Well I certainly have no wish to be married to you!" the Duke rejoined angrily.

The temper which he had kept under control all day seemed to boil over, so that he could no longer prevent himself from adding:

"An irritating, impulsive, half-witted chit is not the type of wife I require. Of that I can assure you!"

He spoke so loudly that his voice seemed to echo round the room and Jabina sprang to her feet.

"How dare you speak to me like that!" she said, her voice as furious as his had been.

"It might do you good to hear the truth for once!" the Duke snapped. "I can assure you, you have nothing to be conceited about, nor have you a priority in insults!"

Jabina made a sound half of fury and half of exasperation and ran out of the parlour.

She slammed the door behind her so violently that the bottles rattled together on the sideboard and a picture which hung on a side wall fell crashing to the ground.

The Duke got to his feet, then sat down again to stare disconsolately into the fire.

'What is the point of raging?' he asked himself.

All the insults and abuse they might hurl at each other's heads would not undo the fact that they were legally married.

He could not imagine two people who were more incompatible.

Jabina had said there must be a way out. He certainly hoped there was. He would have to find a Lawyer and take legal advice on the matter.

He visualised a long series of meetings and arguments, of Lawyers contradicting and opposing each other.

He was appalled at the thought of the publicity it would evoke, and could imagine the laughter of his friends. How amused they would be!

"Poor Drue! Caught at last!" they would cry.

It would be a magnificent jest to recount how he had been ensnared into marriage when he was least expecting it, and not by one of the Socialites who had angled for him in the past but by an unknown Scots wench of whom no-one had even heard.

'The only thing I can do is to behave with dignity,' the Duke thought.

He felt somewhat ashamed that he had let his temper get the better of him when he had raged at Jabina.

But she had needled him once too often by telling him—what he knew already—that he was dull, and the description of his being 'stuck-in-the mud' was the last straw!

"You are in a rut! Your life is monotonous! You will become a bore!"

How often had Freddie and his other friends repeated those warnings!

And now he had been told it again by a mere chit of a girl.

'What does it matter if it is true?' the Duke asked himself but somehow he could not find a convincing reply to his own question.

Realising that his glass was empty, he crossed the room to fill it again from the bottle which had been left on the sideboard. That too was empty!

Impatiently he dragged at the bell-pull and after a moment the door opened and the Inn-keeper's wife stood there.

"Ask your husband to bring me another bottle of wine," the Duke ordered.

"Very good, Your Grace," the woman answered, then added reprovingly: " 'Tis not right that a young lady should be agoing out in the cold at this time o' th'night. She'll get her feet wet and there're some unsavoury characters ahanging around th'Taverns."

The Duke stared at her incredulously. Then he asked:

"Are you telling me that my—s-sister has gone for a walk?"

"I sees her with me own eyes agoing doen th'street some minutes ago," the Inn-keeper's wife replied. "Your Grace shouldn't allow it."

The woman spoke in the stern tones of a Nanny reproving an older child for not attending to a younger one. The Duke rose to his feet.

"I will fetch her back."

Outside the parlour door his fur-lined cloak was hanging on a hook where it had been placed when he first arrived.

As he took it down he noticed that the dark cape that Jabina had been wearing was missing.

He opened the door of the Inn.

Immediately there was a rush of cold air against his face, and he realised that the wind which had abated a little during the day was now blowing hard again and it was very cold.

He stepped out into the street.

It was narrow, with a few scattered houses built hap-hazardly on either side of it and several shops that were now closed and shuttered. At the top of the village was the Kirk.

A little way along the road were several brightly lit windows that the Duke guessed were cheap Taverns where the local inhabitants did their drinking.

The road was rough and slippery under foot.

The Duke set off in the direction that he felt Jabina must have gone, and after walking some little way he thought in the darkness ahead he could see two figures.

As he looked towards them he heard Jabina scream.

On leaving the parlour Jabina had been in such a temper that she had decided in her usual impulsive fashion that she would leave the Duke and never see him again.

She had felt insulted and humiliated because he had refused to speak to her all day, and then when he had raged at her she felt suddenly that she could bear it no longer.

She hated him! She certainly had no intention of staying to listen to his insults, and indeed why should she?

She had come into his life by sheer chance. She would now leave it, and whether they were married or not they need never see each other again.

She was well aware of the value of her mother's jewellery, and when she had changed her dress she had pinned it inside the fresh gown.

She knew it could be dangerous to leave it in her bed-room, and Jabina was cautious enough to have no intention of parting from her one source of wealth until she was safe in her Aunt's home.

In her reticule she carried the fifteen pounds which were still intact, having removed them from the leather bag she carried in the daytime and which she put under her pillow at night.

She was aware that travellers on the open road, and indeed even guests in private houses, had their valuables stolen from them either at night when they were asleep or by more violent methods during the day.

For the first time in her life Jabina felt independent. She had never in the past handled any money of her own, for her father felt there was no necessity for her to have any.

Fifteen pounds seemed to her an enormous sum, and she was speculating that her mother's jewellery, which included a number of quite large stones, would be worth what was to all intents a small fortune.

She would therefore not arrive empty-handed to live

with her Aunt, and perhaps it was the French part of her blood which made her certain that this was important.

No-one wanted an improverished young woman thrust upon them, but one who could pay her way would be welcome and at least not have to play the part of an encumbrance.

Outside the parlour door Jabina had snatched up her travelling-cape and thrown it over her shoulders Pulling the hood over her head, she had opened the door of the Inn and stepped into the street.

Like the Duke, she had felt the sharpness of the wind like a blow, but she was too angry to be checked by anything so trivial.

Neither did she remember that she was not wearing the stout shoes in which she had travelled, but a pair of satin slippers held elegantly across the instep by a single strap which fastened with a small diamante buckle

The coldness of the frost seemed to rise up from the ground and grab her like an icy hand round her ankles.

Jabina was almost running in her eagerness to get away from the Inn and from the Duke, warmed for a moment by the flame of anger inside her and the sound of his jeering, disagreeable voice echoing in her ears.

She walked the whole length of the village street.

She passed the Kirk, and was setting off down the road which seemed to stretch away into an endless darkness when she heard raucous laughter coming from the lighted window of a house standing back a little from the road-side.

A door opened to admit a tall figure wearing a kilt.

Jabina just glanced in the direction of the man leaving what was obviously a Tavern and hurried on.

It was not completely dark, for there was a pale moon creeping up the sky and the stars were already brilliant.

She had not gone very far when she heard footsteps behind her and a voice asked:

"Whither awa', Lassie?"

She turned her head and saw the tall Scot a few paces behind her and decided not to reply.

He caught up with her in three strides.

"Oi' asked ye a question," he said, "an'Oi expects a civil answer."

She knew by the slurring of his voice and the smell of spirits on his breath that he had been drinking.

She tried to move faster but with his long legs he easily kept pace with her.

"Will ye no give a puir mon a penny or two for a drink?" he enquired.

"I should think you have had enough already," Jabina replied.

"Oi've had but one ale," the man cried. "Och, dunna be hard-hearted! Help a countryman in distress."

Thinking she might be rid of him more easily, Jabina stood still.

"If I give you the price of a drink," she asked, "will you leave me alone?"

"Och aye. Oi'll do that," he answered. "All Oi ask is that Oi can wet me whistle."

Jabina opened her reticule.

She remembered that besides the fiften pounds she also had a sixpenny piece and a fourpenny bit that had been lying loose in the House-keeper's money box.

She was feeling for them with her hand inside the reticule when suddenly the bag was snatched from her.

"Oi'll have it noo," he said thickly. "Oi canna be awaiting all night."

"No! No!" Jabina cried, clutching at her bag, but it was too late. He had it in his hands.

Now as she screamed at him he started running down the road away from her, moving so quickly there was no chance of her catching him.

"Stop! Stop!" she screamed, and in trying to run she slipped and fell down on the hard ground.

"Stop!" she screamed again.

Then someone was pulling her to her feet and she realised it was the Duke.

"That man has taken my reticule with all my money in it," she cried. "Catch him! Please catch him!"

"I doubt if anyone could catch him now," the Duke replied. "What the devil do you think you are doing coming out here alone?"

"I was . . . going away."

"How can you be so ridiculous?" the Duke asked. "Come back to the Inn."

"But I have no money," she said plaintively. "That man snatched it from me."

"What did you expect if you walk about the streets in the middle of the night?"

"I was going to give him sixpence," Jabina murmured.

The Duke had turned her round to face the Inn and now, with his arm around her shoulders, they walked back together, finding it hard to keep their footing on the slippery ground.

Finally they reached the Inn.

As they opened the door it was to find the Innkeeper's wife standing in the passage.

She took one look at Jabina's white, unhappy face, then ushered her into the parlour.

"Your feet are soaked through," she said scoldingly. "Now sit down in front of th' fire, M'Lady, and get warm. I'll bring ye a hot toddy, otherwise ye'll be down with a chill tomorrow as sure as I'm standing here."

Meekly Jabina did as she was told. She felt her cloak taken from her and then looked down at her feet to see that her satin slippers were saturated from the snow and frost.

She suddenly realised how cold she was and, as she bent forward to unfasten the strap over her instep, it seemed impossible to make her small fingers do what she required of them.

"Let me do it," the Duke said.

Suddenly he knelt down beside her and was undoing the strap. He took off the first slipper and saw that the stocking beneath it was also wet.

"Slip off your stockings," he said. "You will catch a frightful cold otherwise."

Obediently Jabina lifted the hem of her dress and rolled down her stocking from where it was held by a rather frivolous small blue garter beneath the knee.

The Duke pulled the stocking from her foot and turned his attention to the other one.

As he unfastened the strap and Jabina pushed down her stocking he felt something warm and wet fall on his hand. It was followed by another tear.

When he had taken off the second stocking he lifted Jabina's small foot into his hands. It was very small and pretty, but it was icy cold against the warmth of his fingers.

It had a high, aristocratic instep and each small toe was slightly pink at the end. He rubbed it vigorously, then turned to the other foot.

"Is that better?" he asked, feeling the blood coming back into her feet.

"Yes . . . thank you," she answered in a voice so low he could hardly hear her.

"Why were you running away?" he asked.

"You . . . you were so . . . cross."

"And now it is my turn to apologise," the Duke answered. "I am sorry, Jabina. I do not wish to be so unpleasant."

"You . . . were right . . . to be . . . angry," she murmured.

"Nevertheless I should not have said the things I did."

He looked up at her and their eyes met.

Hers were swimming with unshed tears and he saw that her lips were trembling.

He was about to say something when the door opened and the Inn-keeper's wife came into the room.

She carried a small silver tray on which reposed a glass.

"Now here's your hot toddy, M'Lady," she said, sounding even more like an authoritative Nanny. "Drink up every drop! Otherwise we'll have ye in bed tomorrow with a cold on your chest and coughing your heart up."

Putting the glass into Jabina's cold hands, she watched her take a sip. It was sweet and tasted of honey.

"Drink it all," the Inn-keeper's wife admonished. "I'm agoing to put a bed-warmer in your bed. And the sooner ye get between th'sheets, M'Lady, th'better!"

The Duke rose to his feet.

"Yes, indeed," he said quietly. "And everything will seem different after a good night's rest."

Jabina did not answer him and he had the impression that she was fighting her tears.

She sipped the toddy until she had drained the glass, which he took from her and put on the table.

The door opened and a mob-capped maid put her head into the room.

"Mistress says th'bed be warm an' will Her Ladyship come up reit away?"

She shut the door again and the Duke turned to Jabina with a smile.

It was the first time he had smiled that day.

"You have had your orders!" he said. "I am sure you had better obey them!"

"Y-yes," she murmured.

Then as he turned to pour himself a drink from the fresh bottle of claret that had been set on the side-table, she gave a little exclamation.

"What is it?" the Duke asked.

"I . . . I do not . . . think I can . . . walk!" she answered. "I feel . . . rather . . . strange."

The Duke gave a little laugh.

"And I always thought the Scots could carry their whisky! Come along. I will take you to bed."

He picked her up in his arms. She was very light and her head rested weakly against his shoulder.

"I think . . . I must be . . . botsky!"

"If you are, it will keep out the cold," the Duke answered.

He carried her through the parlour and up the stairs to the low-ceilinged bed-room.

Very gently he set her down on the bed.

"Get into bed as soon as you are undressed, Jabina," he said. "Tomorrow we will try to make plans, but tonight do not trouble over anything."

She looked up at him, her grey-green eyes very worried in her small face.

"I . . . I did not mean . . . to be such a . . . trouble . . ." she murmured.

Chapter Four

The yacht was running before the wind, and never, Jabina thought, had she believed it possible for there to be so much noise.

There was the crack of the wind in the sails, the rasp of the ropes, the cries of command, the running of feet overhead, and the roar of the sea as the bow slipped through the green waves which splashed high over the sides of the ship.

Jabina had never been to sea before and she had not known that it could be so exhilarating, so wildly exciting.

She had always imagined that ships with their high masts and full-bellied sails skimmed serene and steady over the water.

She had therefore been quite unprepared for the pitching and tossing she had endured when first *The Sea Lion* came out of the harbour at Berwick-on-Tweed and into the North Sea.

To her delight she had not been sea-sick. But she found that sailing in the Duke's yacht could be physically exhausting.

There was not only the difficulty of retaining one's balance, but also as the ship altered course the likelihood of being flung roughly on the floor or against the sides of the cabin. On deck there was always the danger of being swept overboard.

Jabina had not expected the Duke's yacht to be so large or indeed so luxurious.

Its masts were high with a bewildering multitude of different sails, and it was manned by forty men, all, the Duke had told her, experienced sea-men.

Below, the cabins were furnished very comfortably and with luxurious taste which Jabina thought was out of keeping with the austerity that the Duke appeared to prefer in his own appearance.

The soft carpets, comfortable beds, and deep arm-chairs, together with the colourful décor left her with the idea that Warminster House would be in fact far more impressive than its owner.

She had however told herself that, whatever she felt or thought, she must not voice her opinions or criticise the Duke.

She was well aware that his temper had been aroused not only by the fact of their unexpected marriage, but also by her remarks and the manner in which she had jibed at him.

She had in fact deserved his sharp retorts which made her do something so foolish as to run away alone into the night.

She felt she had certainly been punished for her be-haviour by losing her money.

She was Scottish enough to regret bitterly that she no longer had fifteen pounds in her handbag. She could only be thankful that at least she had been sensible enough to pin her jewellery inside her dress rather than carry it. That alone now ensured that she was still in-dependent of charity.

The following morning after the Duke had put her to bed, she had come downstairs to the parlour some-what apprehensively.

She thought he might still be angry, perhaps now even more disgusted with her seeing that the whisky she had drunk in the hot toddy had gone to her head.

But to her relief the Duke smiled at her when she appeared at the door, and she felt unaccountably as if the sun had come out.

As they ate their breakfast the Duke had said:

"I have been thinking about the situation in which

we find ourselves, Jabina, and I am convinced there is only one solution."

"And what is . . . that?" Jabina asked nervously.

She had for the moment a panic-stricken fear that he might after all have decided to take her to the Sheriff who would return her to her father.

"I propose," the Duke answered quietly, "to conduct you to the South of France to your Aunt."

Jabina's eyes were wide with surprise, and then she said, a warmth coming into her voice:

"Do you really mean that? You will take me to my Aunt Elspeth?"

"That is what I intend to do," the Duke replied.

"Oh, thank you! Thank you!" Jabina cried. "I was thinking this morning when I first awoke that perhaps I would not be able to manage alone as well as I thought I could."

"Of course you could not do that journey unaccompanied!" the Duke said. "What occurred last night was only one of the unpleasant things that might happen to you."

"I see now I was very . . . foolish!" Jabina said in a humble tone.

The Duke looked at her, noting that her eye-lashes were dark against her cheeks.

He had the feeling that perhaps for the first time in her life Jabina was frightened of the unknown world.

Never in the sheltered existence she had lived with her father had she encountered the harsh realities which would await a young woman who was not protected by a man.

"What I have planned," the Duke went on, "is that we will board my yacht at Berwick-on-Tweed and sail direct to Calais. From there we will travel by road to Nice."

"That sounds wonderful!" Jabina said. "But are you quite sure I am not inconveniencing you too greatly?"

The Duke smiled.

"I really have little alternative," he said. "I can hardly leave you stranded in the North of England, and quite frankly I have no desire to face the problems which would await us in Scotland."

Jabina did not reply and after a moment he continued:

"But I think our Hostess last night solved one problem for us. You will travel as my sister."

"You have no sister?" Jabina asked.

"I am an only child," the Duke replied, "as you are."

"And when we . . . reach my Aunt . . . ?" Jabina asked hesitatingly.

"By then we shall have had time to think," the Duke said, "and perhaps discover if there is a way out of the very unusual predicament in which we find ourselves. For the moment you will be Lady Jabina Minster, and that is the name by which I shall introduce you on board my yacht."

It was fortunate that the Duke's coachmen met no-one from *The Sea Lion,* because they had been told to journey South back to Warminster as soon as the Duke and Jabina left them.

On *The Sea Lion* the Captain, who had once served in the Royal Navy, showed no surprise at being introduced to the Duke's 'sister' although Jabina fancied that he and all the crew were astonished that they should have a lady on board.

The Duke explained this to Jabina later in the evening when they were dining together.

"I have always refused to carry females on *The Sea Lion!"*

"Why?" Jabina enquired.

"Quite frankly, I thought they would be a nuisance," he replied. "Women are usually sea-sick, and what is more they find it impossible to put up with even minor discomforts such as are bound to arise at sea."

"You appear to have a very poor opinion of women!" Jabina exclaimed.

The Duke did not reply for a moment and she said quickly:

"All right, I will say it for you! I have not exactly enhanced your estimation of them."

The Duke laughed.

"The most disarming thing about you, Jabina," he said, "is your frankness."

"In other words you are telling me not to say what I think!" Jabina retorted.

"It is a frightening idea that you might!" he teased.

She realised that as soon as he had come aboard his ship he seemed more relaxed.

She knew too that he was enjoying every moment of the roughness of the sea and the way in which the yacht, which had been specially built for speed, was standing up to the buffeting and the violence of the waves.

'I suppose,' Jabina thought to herself, 'it is a challenge. Perhaps the reason why he finds life so dull is that things are too soft and easy for him.'

She remembered all that Lady McCairn had told her about the Duke's great wealth, his properties not only at Warminster but in other parts of the country, and she decided in her own mind that what the Duke needed was waking up.

She could not know that the Duke's friends had thought just the same thing.

At any rate with the wind ruffling his hair, his face growing tanned from the sun and sharpness of the weather, and wearing oil-skins, the Duke appeared very different from the sober, serious-faced young man who had read a book beside her in the coach.

Jabina had expected them to have interesting conversations at meals, but this she found was almost impossible. At the rate they were travelling and the angle of the ship they could hardly even eat conventionally.

More often than not a dish from which they were helping themselves would be dropped on the floor or slip off the table or be swept from the steward's hands as he staggered and fell back against the side of the cabin.

"If we do not learn to grab our food quickly," Jabina said, "we will starve to death long before we reach Calais!"

At the same time it was all rather fun, and what they did manage to eat tasted delicious because they were both so hungry.

Jabina found herself laughing as their plates and dishes slid about and they could get a drink only by emptying the glass as soon as it was filled.

What was more, the exertion demanded during the day made her so tired at night that she slept the moment her head touched the pillow.

Even if the bed had not been so comfortable, she had the idea she would have slept just as soundly on the floor or anywhere else she could remain without being tossed about.

"Shall I tell you that I am revising my condemnation of women on shipboard?" the Duke asked one evening as they were going to bed.

"I have not been too much of a nuisance?" Jabina enquired.

"You have been admirable in every way," the Duke answered.

There was something in his voice which made her feel shy.

"Be careful!" she admonished. "If you encourage me, I shall doubtless knock down a mast by mistake, or make a hole in the boat with my nail-scissors."

"I think I am immune to surprises by now!" the Duke smiled.

As he spoke the Captain put the yacht about and Jabina was flung into his arms. As she was holding a cup of tea in her hands it was splashed all over him.

"I believe you did that on purpose," the Duke exclaimed as he steadied her.

"You challenged the Fates!" she answered. "Look out for something worse!"

"You are frightening me!" the Duke declared.

He took his arms from her and as he did so Jabina looked up at him mischievously. She thought there was an unusual expression in his eyes as he looked down at her.

Quite unaccountably it was difficult to breathe and Jabina felt something she could not explain constrict her throat. She waited for him to speak.

"Good-night, Jabina," the Duke said gravely, and before she could reply he had left the cabin.

The North wind was behind them all the way to the Channel, and when finally they reached Calais it was to learn from the Captain that they had created a record!

"I am quite sorry to leave the sea," Jabina told the Duke. "At the same time I am very excited at the thought of seeing Paris."

"Do you speak French?" he enquired.

"Are you insulting me?" Jabina retorted. "I told you that my mother was half French and she was very insistent ever since I was a small child that I should acquire a French accent and be so proficient in the language that I would find it as easy as speaking English."

The first night they anchored in Calais harbour they slept on board.

The Duke took Jabina ashore with him while he was making arrangements to hire a carriage and horses to convey them on the next part of their journey.

She listened to him speaking to the Frenchmen in charge of the Livery Stables and was surprised at his extremely good command of the French tongue.

She should have expected, she thought, that with all his learning he would be proficient in the language.

At the same time she realised that his accent was exceptionally good and he had a vocabulary that she had not thought possible for an Englishman.

What was more, she was interested to note that the Duke was a hard bargainer.

When it came to horseflesh he was extremely knowledgeable and refused a number of horses before finally choosing those he required.

When he had completed his business arrangements

he took Jabina to the *Hotel de l'Angleterre,* which he told her Monsieur Dessin had made famous at the end of the last century.

It was in fact the Proprietor who was the owner of the horses and carriage for which the Duke had been negotiating.

"As well as keeping an excellent and expensive table," the Duke said, "our Host sells and hires carriages, changes money, and is said to have already made a fortune of over fifty thousand pounds."

"How do you know all this?" Jabina asked.

"I travelled in France a great deal before the war. Everyone stays at *Dessin's,* as it is more usually called. All the Grand Tourists make it their first port of call."

Jabina looked around her with interest.

There were eight other Englishmen in the Dining-Room who had just crossed the Channel and by eavesdropping on their conversation she gathered that they had come to France with the intention of travelling through Europe to Greece.

They were very noisy at supper, repeatedly calling out, "Wine! Wine! The very best! *Du meilleur! Du meilleur!*" But Monsieur Dessin himself quieted them and offered them the best of his cognac, which they accepted with delight.

The food, Jabina found, was delicious, and what the Duke told her was the *spécialité de la maison,* a dish made with fresh sea-crabs, was something she had never tasted before.

She might be impressed by *Dessin's,* but Calais was disappointing. It was a small town and most of the houses were low and looked bleak and poor.

But what Jabina was to discover both at Calais and on the whole journey to Paris was that the French people not only looked charming but were vastly obliging to strangers.

Never, she thought, had she met such politeness or affability.

Everything was done with such grace and she was extremely impressed even by the beggars.

A boy of about ten years of age asked the Duke for alms. When he refused, thinking that to give to one would cause him to be overwhelmed with the pleading of others, the boy bowed, saying politely:

"Pardon, Monsieur, une autre occasion."

After they had said good-bye to the Captain and crew of *The Sea Lion* Jabina stepped ashore the next morning to find there was quite a cavalcade awaiting her.

The Duke had engaged a *cabriolet* which he could drive himself with two spirited-looking horses. A groom sat behind and was ready to take the reins if required.

And there were also two out-riders, which made Jabina raise her eye-brows in surprise.

"You wished me to travel impressively!" the Duke said with a note of amusement in his voice.

"You did this for me?" Jabina enquired.

"To be truthful," he replied, "our out-riders are really a protection. Travellers can often be robbed on foreign roads, and I am informed that both men are very proficient with the pistol!"

They certainly looked very smart, wearing white wigs and peaked caps of velvet, with a colourful livery which Jabina guessed was far more ostentatious than the Duke would have chosen for his own servants.

There was also a third rider in attendance who, Jabina learned, was to go ahead and order their meals for luncheon and their accommodation for the night.

When finally they set off, the Duke driving with an expertise which she could not help admiring, Jabina felt excitedly that this was the beginning of a great adventure.

As they moved through Calais there was quite a lot of traffic in the streets. The average traveller, the Duke told her, had to choose between a *carrosse,* a *coche,* or a *diligence.*

The *carrosse* was a vehicle like an English stage-coach. The *coche* was larger and heavier, carrying sixteen passengers, twelve in the body of the coach and two on the side of it by the door.

Both, Jabina noticed, carried a great deal more baggage than an English or a Scottish stage-coach.

The *coche* was equipped with two large wicker baskets, one at the front and one at the back, which were overflowing with trunks and bags, boxes and cages, and even in some instances with additional passengers.

Having passed two of these vehicles, Jabina said in a rather shocked voice:

"Surely they are pulled by very small horses and very over-loaded?"

"Lord Nelson called them 'rats of horses,' " the Duke answered. "You will find that the French, for all their charming manners, are often very cruel to animals."

On the way out of Calais they passed a *diligence,* a big public coach whose horses, Jabina learned, were changed every twelve miles as they went at a gallop.

The *diligence* could carry up to thirty passengers all facing the front and could cover as many as a hundred miles a day.

"You can be grateful," the Duke said, "that we are not travelling by *diligence.* They are always very crowded, badly sprung, and they have a habit of starting off in the small hours of the morning!"

"Again I think they over-load the horses," Jabina said severely.

"I agree with you," the Duke answered, "but there is nothing we can do about it."

Once out of the town the Duke had a choice of two roads by which to cover the hundred and eighty-three miles to Paris.

The *carrosse* route, which was the worst, went through Abbeville, Beauvais, and Beaumont.

"Most of the Inns on that road are atrocious!" the Duke said.

He took the post-route which went through Amiens, Clermont, and Chantilly, and the first Inn at which they stayed was pleasant, and the food if not exotic was palatable.

The Inn-keepers both at lunch and supper, Jabina

found, were courteous and well-mannered and she found everything en route an enchantment.

There were none of the villain *sansculottes* of Gilray's cartoons to be seen, but friendly faces and on the whole well-dressed citizens.

The women in the market-places, in their red camlet jackets and high aprons, with long flying lappets to their caps and wooden sabots, were entrancing.

And Jabina loved the markets themselves, with their gay painted eggs and mounds of butter and the long crisp rolls of new baked bread on the stalls and the tang of garlic in the air.

At the Inn where they slept, they enjoyed what the Duke said was a typical French dinner. There was soup served by the Landlord and a fish course.

After there was duck with cucumber, tongue with tomato sauce, and *fricandeau* of veal.

When these dishes were removed, there were sweetmeats, puddings, stewed and fresh fruit, and cakes.

What Jabina did notice with surprise was that once they were out of the towns and driving through the open country they hardly ever saw a man.

Instead there were blackened and sun-burnt women with bare heads or their hair covered with handkerchiefs working in the fields.

"Napoleon has not relaxed his recruitment of the Army!" the Duke explained.

"But we have!"

"Yes, indeed, we have disbanded whole regiments—halved the number of men in the Navy and laid up a number of ships. It is crazy!"

"Crazy?" Jabina questioned. "You do not think that we will go to war again? I thought that it was over!"

"They were saying in Calais that things are very tense in diplomatic circles," the Duke answered, "but we shall learn more when we reach Paris."

"There were so many men killed before the Armistice," Jabina said in a low voice. "I cannot believe that Napoleon Bonaparte wants to fight England."

"If he could conquer us he would!" the Duke said. "Make no mistake about that! The difficulty as far as he is concerned is that he must cross the Channel to do it!"

"But if we went to war again," Jabina said in a low voice, "I should be living in an enemy country."

"As your Aunt has done these last years," the Duke replied.

"But she is married to a Frenchman. She therefore takes his nationality," Jabina said.

This was unanswerable and they drove on in silence.

With her usual buoyancy Jabina thought that the Duke must be unduly anxious.

After all, everyone had said when the Armistice came that war between their two countries was finished for all time.

At Amiens and again at Chantilly the Duke found there were people already predicting that England and France would be at each other's throats in a month's time.

It seemed impossible in the May sunshine with the Spring flowers all along the road-sides, the trees in bloom and the warmth of the sun making them discard their heavy coats, to imagine the horrors of war.

Dangers, like the snow, seemed to have been left behind, and when they reached Chantilly on the sixteenth of May Jabina was trying to persuade the Duke to stay several days in Paris before they set out for the South.

"I have always been told it is such a gay city. Please . . . please let me see a little of it before we go any further," she pleaded.

The Duke had not allowed her to visit any of the Castles or the Churches on the post-route, saying that he was in a hurry to reach Paris as soon as possible.

She had the feeling that it was rather because he was worried about the political situation than that he wished to be rid of her.

Because she was so interested they had, while they were in Chantilly, visited the famous gardens of the Prince de Conde. The canals, waterfalls, and fountains

78

had been laid waste after the Revolution, but now restoration had been put in hand.

There were aviaries of exotic birds almost hidden in the groves and Jabina was enthralled by everything she saw.

When they reached St. Denis she persuaded the Duke to show her the Benedictine Abbey, where the French Crown Jewels were kept.

She was disappointed with Charlemagne's golden crown, which to her did not seem grand enough, but his diamond-encrusted sword and ivory chessmen lived up to her expectations.

There was also a nail from the cross of Christ, a crucifix made of the true wood of the cross carved by Pope Clement III, a box in which was some of the Virgin's hair and one of the thorns which the Monks said had been in the crown worn by Jesus at his crucifixion.

"Fancy their having been kept safely all down the centuries!" Jabina exclaimed breathlessly to the Duke.

He did not attempt to disillusion her in words, but she knew by the twist of his lips that he did not really believe that such relics were authentic.

The entrance into Paris was beset with formalities and hindrances.

There were iron gates and a barrier stretching across the road and once they had passed these, the Customs' Officers in the *Bureau de Roi* examined every part of the *post-chaise* as well as Jabina's and the Duke's baggage for forbidden articles.

While the searching was going on they were besieged by elegantly-dressed young men who pleaded in broken English to be employed as valets.

They thrust into the *cabriolet* references written in English by their previous employers.

The Duke waved them away with an authority which they somewhat reluctantly obeyed.

"Where are we staying?" Jabina asked as they set off again.

The Customs' Officers had to their disappointment found nothing that was contraband.

"The best Hotels are in the Faubourg St. Germain, but I have sent our courier ahead to see if he can take us furnished rooms which are far more comfortable. It is the way I have always stayed when I have been in Paris and I am sure he will find us a place in the same locality."

Sure enough the Duke was not to be disappointed.

The rooms which covered the first and second floor of a large mansion which had once been owned by an Aristocrat were in Jabina's opinion extremely luxurious.

She was cheered by the thought that as the Duke had taken private rooms rather than stay at a Hotel it must mean that he intended to give in to her pleadings to stay for a few days, perhaps even a week, in Paris.

She had already seen as she entered the Capital a number of open-air dancing places, and as they drove along the roads she could hear the sound of the violin, clarinet, and tambourine.

"They dance like maniacs in Paris, M'mselle," one of the chambermaids had told her at Chantilly. "It is dance, dance day and night! It is all Parisiennes think about!"

The woman had spoken scornfully because she was getting on in years, but to Jabina it was an excitement she had not expected.

Now she was wondering how she could persuade the Duke to take her dancing, but somehow she could not imagine him finding a plebeian Dance-Hall amusing.

They had hardly been in their rooms an hour when to Jabina's astonishment tradesmen came knocking on the door.

The valet whom the Duke had engaged with the apartment and the maid who was to look after Jabina spent their time answering them.

Tailors, perruquiers, hatters, shoe-makers, seamstresses, gown-makers, jewellers, every type of salesman concerned with clothes for gentlemen and ladies, called in quick succession.

Jabina thought the Duke might turn them away without even listening to what they had to say.

Then as she looked pleadingly at him he realised as if for the first time how unfashionable her clothes were.

He really had not concerned himself with what Jabina was wearing.

Now he realised she could have carried very little in the small trunk which was all she had brought with her when she escaped from her father's house.

It seemed to the Duke, as he thought about it, that she had in fact worn the same gown day after day and the same evening-gown every night.

When lengths of silk and muslin, gauze and lace were rolled out for his inspection he understood how much they meant to a woman—any woman—and perhaps especially to Jabina.

He picked out a *couturier* and said firmly:

"I want six fashionable gowns for M'mselle. One must be ready for her to wear tonight. Another for tomorrow morning."

Jabina gave a little cry of sheer excitement.

"Do you mean it? Do you really mean it?" she asked.

Then as a sudden thought struck her she drew him a little to one side, where the people flowing into the Salon could not hear her.

"I . . . I must not spend too much!" she said in a low voice. "I do not know yet how much my mother's jewellery will fetch when I sell it."

"What I have ordered for you is a present, Jabina," the Duke replied.

The light in her eyes was almost dazzling.

"Thank you! Thank you a thousand, million times!" she said. "May I choose anything I like?"

"These people will have sketches with them," he said, "and perhaps even a model. I do not wish to question your taste, Jabina, but I would like to choose them with you."

"Yes, yes of course!" she agreed.

She hurried into her bed-chamber, followed by the

Parisiennes carrying their goods, talking volubly and advising her which were the most alluring styles.

It seemed incredible to Jabina, but by the evening her gown was ready.

She had a suspicion that much of it must have been made before her arrival, but nevertheless it fitted her perfectly and for the first time in her life she realised she had an attractive figure.

The full-skirted gowns with their muslin fichus she had worn in Scotland were decidedly out of date.

Josephine Bonaparte, wife of the First Consul, had introduced a style to Paris which had, Jabina learnt, been accepted by those in the fashion.

The gowns falling straight from a high waist were almost transparent, revealing the curve of the hips and accentuating the breasts.

The neckline was cut very low and the tiny little puffed-sleeves over the shoulders were often ornamented with diamanté and trimmed with lace.

Jabina's gown was of white gauze with a fine thread of silver woven into it which glittered and shone when she moved. Silken ribbons crossed over the bodice and tied at the back. Slippers to match the gown were of silver.

A *coiffeuse* arranged her red hair in what was almost a Grecian style with ringlets falling from the back.

When she stared at herself in the mirror she could hardly believe that she was really seeing the reflection of Jabina Kincarthie and not some glamorous, alluring stranger.

The Duke had promised to take her out to dinner and she wondered what he would say when he saw her.

She was a little afraid that he might be shocked that her figure was so openly revealed, and yet not for all the disapproval in the world would she have asked for another thickness to be added to the gown.

When her maid had at last finished dressing her, Jabina put on her mother's diamond necklace and clasped a matching diamond bracelet round her wrist.

"Your velvet wrap is ready for you, M'mselle," the maid said.

"I will not put it on for the moment," Jabina answered. "I want to show my brother my new dress. Is he in the Salon?"

"His Grace has just left his bed-chamber, M'mselle. He is helping himself to a glass of wine," the maid reported, having peeped through a crack in the door.

Jabina took a last look at herself in the mirror.

"Open the door for me, Yvette," she ordered and walked forward.

Jabina entered the salon and stood for a moment in the doorway waiting for the Duke to notice her.

When he turned from the side-table she let out an exclamation of sheer astonishment.

"Oh . . . !"

For a moment she could hardly believe her eyes! It was undoubtedly the Duke, but changed almost out of recognition.

Gone was the dreary black suit, the low, neatly tied cravat, and the unfashionable hair-style.

Instead a Buck—a Dandy—a *Petit Maître* stood in front of her! His high cravat meticulously tied, the points of his collar above the line of his chin.

The dark blue satin coat accentuated his broad shoulders, and the tight, champagne-coloured pantaloons revealed the narrowness of his hips.

A fob hung from his waist-coat, the buttons of which glittered dazzlingly.

"Do you approve?" the Duke asked with a faint smile as Jabina after the first exclamation seemed to have become speechless.

"You look . . . wonderful!" she exclaimed. "I never thought you could look like that! It is fantastic!"

The Duke laughed.

"I am flattered!" he said. "And now let me tell you, although perhaps not so eloquently, that you too look very different!"

"You approve?"

"Decidedly so! I should have told you that French couturières are magicians."

"Of course they are!" Jabina agreed, her eyes dancing, "and we both look supremely elegant and not in the least like the cartoons of English tourists."

"I do not believe we can hide our nationality as easily as that!" the Duke laughed, "but there is no doubt that you look very much a Lady of Fashion!"

"And you are exactly as I wanted you to be!" Jabina said.

The Duke's eyes met hers as if enquiringly. Then before they could say any more a servant opened the door and announced:

"Le Vicomte Armand D'Envier!"

As his name rang out a thin, dark Frenchman came into the room and the Duke gave a loud exclamation of delight.

"Armand!" he exclaimed. "I was hoping you would be in Paris."

"It was just by chance I heard that you had arrived, my dear Drue," the Vicomte replied.

The two men shook hands and then as the Vicomte glanced towards Jabina the Duke said:

"I am accompanied by my sister. Let me introduce you. Jabina—this is a very old friend of mine—Le Vicomte D'Envier—my sister, Lady Jabina Minster."

The Vicomte bowed politely.

"Enchanté, M'mselle! I hope I may have the pleasure of showing you Paris if this is your first visit?"

"It is indeed," Jabina answered.

"Then you must both dine with me now—tonight!" the Vicomte said. "I hope you have no other engagements, Drue, for now that I have found that you have your sister with you, I must tell you that I had every intention of taking you, whether you liked it or not, to a Ball which my Aunt is giving for one of my cousins. You must both come with me. It will be a very amusing evening. Lady Jabina will shine like a meteor among our *demoiselles Parisiennes.*"

"I am not certain if we can manage tonight . . ." the

Duke began, only to be interrupted by Jabina, who laid her hand on his arm.

"Please . . . please let us go," she begged.

There was no doubt that she was longing to be present at the Ball and the Duke yielded to her request.

"Very well, Armand," he said. "Anyway I am sure if I refuse, you will pay no attention. You always have dragged me from one place of amusement to another."

"Tonight I need be concerned not only with your entertainment," the Vicomte said. "There is your sister, who must realise that even under the heel of a coarse Corsican, Paris can still be a city of enchantment."

The Duke laughed.

"Still the Royalist! Still fighting the *Régime,* Armand? Still intent upon overthrowing the little Corporal?"

"Our time will come!" the Vicomte said ominously. "We are making our plans, Drue, to rid ourselves of this *parvenu* who has set himself up not only as a conqueror and ruler of France but also as an arbitor of fashion!"

He spoke almost violently and then he added:

"You will hardly believe it, but Bonaparte has created a new Aristocracy, giving them fancy titles which make those of us who are real Aristocrats and have the bluest blood of France in our veins feel sick at the insult!"

"I cannot allow you to be serious tonight," the Duke said. "Perhaps tomorrow we will feel inclined to take sides and to support you in your fight against Bonaparte, but at the moment I am both hungry and thirsty and Jabina is the same. We travelled very swiftly to get here."

"Now you have arrived there is no hurry," the Vicomte said. "You are right, Drue. Let us forget everything but the joy of being alive and of being in the most beautiful city in the world."

Jabina put on her wrap and the Duke placed an evening-cloak lined with red silk over his shoulders.

Then they went down the wide graceful staircase to the marble Hall below, where a flunky ushered them out to where the Vicomte's coach was waiting.

Paris, Jabina was to notice that night and to learn the next day, was a city of contrasts as well as of speed, noise, and constant activity.

As they drove through the streets they had glimpses of magnificent Churches, Palaces, and large impressive houses which she guessed had belonged to the nobility of the Aristocratic *Régime*.

She saw the wide bridges over the Seine and the beautiful gardens of the Tivoli, but there were also dirty streets pointing to poverty and squalor.

Outside the glittering shops, still open although the evening was drawing on, beside many of the houses there were piles of rotten apples and herrings, sacks, bundles, and filth which appeared to have been lying there not for a day but perhaps for weeks or months.

She had not the time to see much before they arrived at a Restaurant called *Chez Robert,* where the Vicomte told them he always had a table reserved for him.

"You and I have eaten here often in the past," he said to the Duke, "and I suggest we dine here tonight before my Aunt's Ball. I am certain your sister will be interested in sampling the best food in Paris and drinking from what is undoubtedly the best cellar."

If Jabina had not been so entranced by her surroundings she would, she thought later, have been able to give more of her attention to the food and wine.

As it was, she found it difficult to take in everything at once; the elegant French women glittering with diamonds and dressed in such transparent gowns it seemed as if they were completely naked underneath one layer of gauze or muslin.

The men too were dressed flamboyantly and far more elaborately than any Englishman would have thought permissible.

But however smart they might be, Jabina could not help thinking that the Duke was outstanding.

She thought so again when they reached the Ball being given by the Vicomte's Aunt.

From the moment they entered the huge Salon where their Hostess was receiving, Jabina was aware that she was meeting not only families belonging to the ancient *Régime* of France but also the upstarts—the new Sociabilities of whom the Vicomte had spoken so scathingly.

To whichever class they belonged, the women were extremely attractive and had a vivacious gaiety and vitality which was typically French.

There was dancing in a great chandelier-lighted Ball-room and outside in the garden there was a specially laid floor beneath lanterns hung from trees that had just come into blossom.

The formal grounds were illuminated with tiny candlelights which gave the whole place a fairy-like appearance.

Jabina had no lack of partners, but she was piqued that the Duke did not ask her to dance and she would rather have danced with him than anyone else.

But the Vicomte was her partner a number of times until finally late in the evening, or rather early in the morning, she found herself sitting with him in an arbour from where they could watch the dancers moving as gracefully as swans.

"Tell me about yourself," the Vicomte said.

He had a beguiling charm, Jabina decided, which she could imagine many women would have found almost irresistible.

He looked at her ardently with his dark eyes, and yet when he paid her a compliment she could not help feeling that it came automatically to his lips and was too smooth to be completely sincere.

"What do you want to know?" she asked, hoping his questions would not be too inquisitive.

"Well, one thing I am burning to hear," the Vicomte replied, "is how after so many years of being an only child, Drue has suddenly produced a sister!"

Jabina stiffened.

This was something she had not expected. She searched for words but before she could speak the Vicomte went on:

"You can trust me. If it is a liaison which he does not wish to acknowledge, I should be only too delighted!"

"No. It is . . . nothing like . . . that!" Jabina said quickly.

"Then I am sorry," the Vicomte said. "When I saw you in the Salon tonight I thought to myself—at last Drue has seen the error of his ways! At last he had begun to enjoy himself!"

"You do not think he has enjoyed his life in the past?" Jabina asked anxiously.

"Not since he was fifteen," the Vicomte replied.

"What happened then?"

"You do not know?"

"No."

"First tell me about yourself," the Vicomte asked.

"It . . . it is a . . . secret," Jabina said uncomfortably.

"All the more reason why I should know it," the Vicomte replied. "I can of course ask Drue, but I have a feeling it might embarrass him to realise I am not deceived by your pretended relationship."

"I . . . I am not . . . his sister," Jabina said hesitatingly. "I am in fact . . . his wife!"

"His wife?"

There was no doubt that the Vicomte was astonished!

If she had been a little more sophisticated Jabina might have been insulted by what he had obviously believed her to be.

Shyly Jabina told the Vicomte what had happened and how quite inadvertently she and the Duke found themselves married by Scottish law.

When she had finished he clapped his hands together.

"Bravo!" he said. "It is the best thing that could possibly have happened! Drue had sworn he would never get married. Well now it has been forced upon him and it may, in fact I am sure it will, be the saving of him."

"Explain! Please explain to me what you are talking about?" Jabina pleaded.

"He has not told you about his childhood or what happened when he was fifteen?" the Vicomte enquired.

Jabina shook her head.

"I only know that he intended never to be wed. He was angry . . . very angry when he discovered what had happened."

"And now he is taking you to your Aunt to be rid of you," the Vicomte remarked.

"Perhaps I can just disappear out of his life," Jabina said a little wistfully. "There is only Lady McCairn in Scotland to say we are married. If she is told I am dead, what can she do about it?"

"Now listen to me," the Vicomte said. "Drue is one of my oldest friends. I have known him ever since we were at school together and I like him more than any other man I have ever met. Together you and I have to save him from himself."

"But how?" Jabina asked.

The Vicomte looked at her with a little smile on his lips.

"Do you, a woman, really have to ask me a question like that?"

"The Duke hates me!" Jabina said. "He was furious at finding himself married to me and I am everything he most dislikes in a woman. He told me so!"

"And you . . . ?" the Vicomte enquired. "Do you dislike him?"

"I think he is dull and pompous and he is very disagreeable when he pleases," Jabina said quickly.

Then a vision of the Duke as she had seen him tonight with his new cravat holding his chin high, his elegant clothing, and the smile on his lips made her hesitate.

She looked up at the Vicomte, who was watching her.

"I have just . . . realised," she said in a low voice, "that I hardly know him at all. Tell me about him. Tell me . . . everything you know!"

Chapter Five

"I met Drue first," the Vicomte began, "when we were at Eton together."

Jabina's eyes were on his face as he went on:

"My father believed that I should have a cosmopolitan education and sent me to school in England and encouraged me to invite my English friends back to Paris."

"Drue came to Paris?" Jabina asked.

"Several times," the Vicomte replied, "and I stayed with him at Warminster and at his other Estates in England."

He paused for a moment, then went on:

"We were close friends and I think, looking back, that Drue became not only my friend, but the brother I never had."

"Did he feel the same about you?" Jabina enquired.

"I always believed so," the Vicomte answered with a smile.

"And you met his father and mother?" Jabina questioned.

"Of course," the Vicomte replied. "Drue's father was very like him. Charming, courteous, extremely erudite."

"And his mother?"

Jabina felt that here was the key to what the Vicomte had said.

"Drue's mother was one of the most beautiful women I have ever seen in my life!" he replied. "It was not only that her features were classically perfect, but she had a vivacity and gaiety that one does not associate with English women."

He hesitated a moment, as if choosing his words, before he went on:

"But looking back, I think I realised even as a boy that she was very emotional and therefore easily swayed."

"What do you mean by that?" Jabina enquired.

"I am trying to explain to you—perhaps also to myself—the reason why she ran away!"

"Ran away?" Jabina ejaculated.

"With a man younger than herself. A raffish, rather dissolute Peer with whom she fell overwhelmingly in love."

Jabina's eyes were fixed on his face.

"And Drue minded?"

"It hit him like an explosion. I think at first he could hardly believe that his mother had really left his father and him. Even when the tragedy occurred, he still found it hard to credit it."

"What tragedy?" Jabina asked.

"The Duchess of Warminster and Lord Beldon were drowned when the yacht in which they had left England foundered in a squall in the Bay of Biscay."

"How terrible!" Jabina exclaimed.

"I think that, until the moment of her death, Drue's father always believed that his wife would return to him. When there was no hope of that happening, he became a changed man."

"In what way?"

The Vicomte smiled.

"I suppose the answer is that he became very much like Drue is now!"

Jabina did not say anything and he continued:

"At first he was desperately depressed, and I always think Drue, although he has never mentioned it to me, had a very difficult time with his father. Perhaps he even had to prevent him taking his own life."

"Poor Drue!" Jabina murmured beneath her breath.

"Then being compelled to acccept the situation, the Duke withdrew more and more into himself and occupied his time by reading."

"Just like Drue!" Jabina exclaimed.

"At first Drue did not emulate his father. He was away from home at school and later at Oxford where we were again together, and for a time he became very wild."

"I can hardly believe that!"

"It is true, I assure you!" the Vicomte affirmed. "He drank a great deal, gambled, and inevitably like the rest of us he was interested in women."

Jabina drew a deep breath.

This was something she had not expected to hear.

"But his attitude to women was different from mine and that of the rest of his friends," the Vicomte said.

"What was that?" Jabina enquired.

"I think I can explain it by saying that he wished to hurt," the Vicomte answered. "It was as if every time he left a woman weeping or miserable, he revenged himself on his mother."

"I can . . . understand that!"

"I think in a way I did too, but it did not make Drue himself any happier."

"No, of course not."

"He is a kind, generous, and understanding person at heart—he always has been," the Vicomte said, "but during this period he was hard, insensitive, and at times undoubtedly cruel!"

"He must have missed his mother intolerably," Jabina said almost beneath her breath.

"I think the shock of her leaving him was more intense to Drue than it would have been to any ordinary young man," the Vicomte explained. "They were a very united and happy family until this happened."

"How could she have done such a thing?"

"I have often asked myself that question," the Vicomte answered, "and I think it was because she felt in a way she was growing old and that youth was escaping her. She was like a beautiful butterfly. She loved life. She wanted to hold it tight in her arms. She wanted to enjoy everything and miss nothing."

"So she fell in love."

"As I have said, she was very emotional. It is hard for you to understand, having only known Drue as he is now, but he too is capable of very deep feelings."

Jabina looked away across the garden.

"I did not . . . realise that."

"How could you?" the Vicomte asked. "You have never seen him except as he is now. But I am certain of one thing, that holding himself in check as he has these last years, bridling his feelings, damping down his natural emotions, does not mean that the fire within him has burnt out."

The Vicomte paused to say almost prophetically:

"One day it will burst into flame again."

Jabina was silent.

Looking at her serious little face silhouetted against the light of the lanterns, the Vicomte said:

"I am convinced, I always have been, that Drue's present behaviour is merely an act. The real Drue, the one I admire, the one with whom I grew up, lies underneath the austerity, the solemnity, the incredible boredom he has inflicted upon himself."

"I wonder if that is true?"

"I am sure of it," the Vicomte replied, "and that is why I welcome you with open arms into Drue's life. If anyone could save him, it would be you!"

"He hates me!" Jabina cried.

"I very much doubt it," the Vicomte rejoined. "I cannot help suspecting that the reason Drue has changed his appearance for the first time in eight years is that you persuaded him to dress differently."

He gave a little laugh and added:

"What happened to the sombre black which made him look like an undertaker?"

Jabina laughed too and then she explained:

"It only happened today! He arrived in Paris looking, I thought, like a Presbyterian Minister."

"Well, at least this alteration is one step in the right direction," the Vicomte said.

"You have not told me when he changed from being gay, irresponsible, and unkind to women to the repressed, puritanical man I met in Scotland."

"It was after we came down from Oxford," the Vicomte answered. "It was then that I think he realised fully how much his mother had hurt his father."

"It must have been . . . horrible for him," Jabina murmured.

"As I told you," the Vicomte went on, "Drue and his father were basically very much alike, and I think the old Duke clung to his son there being no-one else for whom he cared."

"That is . . . understandable."

"Anyway, instead of joining his friends in London, Drue settled down at Warminster."

"Alone with his father."

"That is right," the Vicomte agreed, "and almost inevitably Drue modelled himself on what his father had become. I stayed with them once and found it almost unbelievable that they would sit talking into the early hours of the morning on some obscure point in Mediaeval literature, or spend days planning minor improvements on the Estate which could quite easily have been left to a farm-manager."

He hesitated as if the words would not come.

"It was almost as if the older man was determined to fill his existence with trivialities and make them a compensation for what he had lost."

"It was his only hope," Jabina said.

"It did not much matter where the old Duke was concerned, but with Drue it was disastrous!" the Vicomte told her. "He became too like his father for it to be funny, and was so much of a bore that many of his friends found him intolerable."

"He still has some friends?" Jabina asked almost pleadingly.

"I will always be Drue's friend," the Vicomte said. "For the last few years I have been separated from him by the Channel. As a Frenchman I could not visit England. But before the war I did not go to Warminster for two years or so, and only received news of him from other friends when they visited Paris, and they had not anything encouraging to tell me."

"I think myself," Jabina said, "that what he needs is a challenge: something against which he will have to battle and thus will be forced out of the groove to which he has condemned himself."

"You have a great deal of sense in that pretty head of yours!" the Vicomte remarked.

Jabina flushed and then laughed.

"I am flattered by your compliments."

"I mean it," the Vicomte said, "and as I said at the beginning, I am certain you are the one person who can save Drue."

"I doubt it," Jabina answered, "but at the same time I am very grateful to you for telling me the truth. I did not understand how he could be as he is."

The Vicomte sighed.

"In France we always suspect a woman to be at the bottom of every problem and difficulty. We say *Cherchez la femme* and we mean it!"

He reached out and took Jabina's hand in his.

"We also believe that where one woman has created a difficult situation, another can put things right. It is up to you, Jabina!"

"I will do my best," Jabina promised, "but I will not be with him for long."

"I think we must both try to persuade Drue to prolong his visit," the Vicomte suggested.

There was a light in Jabina's eyes.

"Do you think you could do that?" she asked. "There is so much I want to see! So much I want to do that is amusing and exciting in this wonderful city. Its people are so gay!"

"I like to hear you say that!" the Vicomte said. "So many of your countrymen have abused mine that it is a delight to hear something nice for a change."

He raised her hand, which he still held in his, to his lips.

"We must go back to Drue," he said, "or he will suspect that I have designs on you. I have no wish to fight a duel with my oldest friend."

"I do not think he would care if you were interested," Jabina said in a low voice. "I think he would be glad to be rid of me."

"I should not be too sure of that!" the Vicomte replied. "At the same time you must make certain that if you do leave him he will miss you more than at the moment seems possible."

"What I am concerned with now," Jabina said, "is that you should persuade him to stay in Paris. Please! Please try!"

"I will certainly do my best and not only for your sake, but also for mine. I cannot tell you what pleasure it is for me to see Drue again and relive the happy times we spent together when we were young."

He gave a little laugh.

"I should not like to tell you of all the escapades in which we took part or indeed the plans we made together for the future. But then neither of us had visualised war between our two countries."

"War!"

Jabina gave a little shiver.

"I have the feeling," she said, "that that is what Drue, when we find him, will be talking about."

They walked back to the house and found, as Jabina suspected, that Drue, standing by the buffet in the Supper-Room, was talking with a number of young men. As they drew near them she heard the word 'Bonaparte' and knew that she had been right in her supposition.

"I wondered what had happened to you both," the Duke said as Jabina and the Vicomte joined him.

He did not sound particularly interested.

"Are you ready to leave? I have my carriage outside," the Vicomte asked.

"I think we are both tired," the Duke replied. "It has been a long day."

"But a very exciting one!" Jabina said quickly.

"There will be many more things to do tomorrow," the Vicomte promised. "Let me take you home and I will call for you in the morning."

"To do what, may I ask?" the Duke enquired.

"See the sights, for one thing," the Vicomte replied. "'Your sister will have to visit the Louvre, the Tivoli Gardens, Notre Dame, and of course the Great High Panjandrum himself—our First Consul!"

The Vicomte's voice sharpened as he spoke of Bonaparte and perhaps to tease him the Duke said:

"I would rather like to meet the man who, whatever else you may say about him, has single-handed united France after the Revolution."

"Not entirely!" the Vicomte snapped.

"No, not entirely," the Duke conceded, "but very nearly! While to us your régime seems a Military despotism, the people of France see Bonaparte as their only defence against the Priests, the Aristocrats, and the foreigners."

"I do not intend to let you needle me into quarrelling with you, Drue," the Vicomte said. "You are like all the idiots who come to Paris to be fascinated by the Common Corsican. I have listened to all of them drooling on about him, and all I can say to you is: try living in France and see what you feel about him then!"

"What concerns me more at the moment," the Duke said in a different tone, "is that everyone I have spoken to so far appears to think that revival of hostilities is inevitable."

"I would not be surprised," the Vicomte replied.

"I have just been told," the Duke went on, "that our Ambassador, Lord Whitchurch, has definitely left for England."

"I wonder if that is true," the Vicomte queried. "There have been so many rumours this past week or so—that he is leaving, then he is not, or that he has left and someone has fetched him back."

He laughed.

"What you have heard may easily be just wishful thinking from those who want England to win our battles for us."

"I very much hope that is true," the Duke said, "but if it is not then Jabina and I ought to return home."

"We will find out tomorrow," the Vicomte said soothingly. "I have friends who are very close to Bonaparte. It is not a position I should wish to be in myself, but at least they will tell me exactly what is in the wind."

"Then let us spend a peaceful night without worrying," the Duke suggested.

They said good-bye to their Hostess and the Vicomte escorted them to his carriage, an elegant vehicle driven by two coachmen with a footman standing up behind.

They stepped in and drove a little way, the Duke and the Vicomte speaking of the past and the parties they had enjoyed when they were young.

Then unexpectedly the carriage stopped not in the Faubourg St. Germain as Jabina had expected it to do, but outside the garishly lighted entrance to what was obviously a Dance-Garden.

The Duke looked out of the window in surprise and the Vicomte said:

"Do you remember this place, Drue? We used to come here often enough. In those days it was called *Le Jardin Du Roi.* Now it has moved with the times and is called *Le Jardin de la Liberté,* but it is still very gay."

"Oh! Could we . . . could we go in for a moment?" Jabina begged.

The Vicomte looked at the Duke with a smile.

"I see no reason why not. It is up to Drue."

"I am sure Jabina would like to see where we misspent our youth," he said.

With a little cry of delight, Jabina jumped out of the carriage as soon as the footman opened the door.

The garden was brilliantly lit with lanterns and there were crowded tables at which people were sitting drinking wine and watching the dancers.

Coming straight from a sedate and elegant Ball, it was impossible not to notice the noise which came both from the orchestra and from the clients.

There was the wild chattering of voices and laughter and even shouts and cheers as those that were dancing sped at an incredible rate around the polished floor.

It was not bawdy or in any way vulgar, just the expression of sheer *joie de vivre*. Jabina listened and watched with shining eyes, feeling more excited than she had the whole evening.

The guests at the Ball had moved to slow, dignified waltzes, French contre-dances, and English gavottes.

In the garden the waltzing was so quick that the couples seemed almost to twirl round the floor, and the other dances in which they indulged were spirited and obviously physically exhausting.

The Vicomte ordered two bottles of wine. It was weak and very inferior to that which they had drunk at the Ball, but Jabina could not help thinking that the atmosphere in the garden was intoxicating enough in itself.

She watched for a little while and then as another waltz struck up she put her hand on the Duke's arm.

"Please, will you dance with me?"

He looked at her in surprise and she thought for a moment that he would refuse.

Then the Vicomte said:

"You used to be rather an expert at the light-fantastic, Drue, or have your feet lost their cunning?"

"Perhaps I had better find out," the Duke replied.

He rose as he spoke and led Jabina onto the dance floor.

She had somehow expected him to be stiff and

clumsy. Instead, to her surprise, he danced exceedingly well, far better than any of her partners at the Ball.

He also held her more closely and she found that she could follow his steps quite easily. In fact they danced together as if it were something they had done a hundred times before.

He whirled her round the floor and she found herself laughing up at him, enjoying the dance far more than she had enjoyed anything the whole evening.

It was difficult to talk since the noise around them was deafening, but it was exciting for Jabina to know that they moved in unison and to be aware that they were undoubtedly the best-dressed and most oustanding couple in the whole garden.

When they returned to the Vicomte he clapped his hands together.

"Bravo!" he cried. "The fair charmers who taught you, Drue, would be proud of you!"

"I think now we should go home," the Duke said.

"Can we come here another evening?" Jabina begged. "It is fun—much more fun than anywhere I have ever been in my whole life!"

"You will find *bastringues* like these all over Paris," the Vicomte said. "You will have to persuade Drue to let you sample them. No-one knows better than he does how amusing they can be!"

The Duke did not answer.

The Vicomte teased him all the way back to the Faubourg St. Germain and the Apartment.

As they stepped out of his carriage he said:

"*Au revoir,* My Lady, until tomorrow. I shall be counting the hours."

"So shall I!" Jabina said gaily. "Thank you for such a wonderful time."

A tired flunky shut the outer door behind them and Jabina and the Duke went up the stone staircase which must once have known the great Aristocrats of France, until they reached the sitting-room of their suite.

"It has been a wonderful evening," she said.

Then, because the Duke did not speak and she felt slightly piqued by his silence, she said:

"I was a huge success! I was—really! Several extremely handsome Frenchmen wished to kiss me!"

"And I presume you allowed them to do so?"

There was an angry note in the Duke's voice which made Jabina start.

Suddenly she remembered all that the Vicomte had told her and realised that perhaps the Duke would think she had been behaving in the way his mother had done.

She saw the scowl between his eyes and quickly she threw out her hands towards him.

"No! No!" she cried. "It is not true!"

"You were lying?" the Duke asked.

"Yes," she answered, "or rather . . . exaggerating. Just one of my partners said when we were dancing that he would like to . . . kiss me because I looked like a child at her first party."

She spoke very quickly, her voice tumbling over the words because she was ashamed and embarrassed at having to explain herself.

It seemed to her that the scowl between the Duke's eyes was still there.

"I was only boasting," she said. "Please do not be angry with me."

"I cannot understand why you should wish to deceive me with such falsehoods," the Duke said in a reproving tone.

Jabina turned a little away from him.

"You never asked me to dance when we were at the Ball," she said. "You never told me that I looked . . . pretty and I . . . wanted you to think I did."

There was a silence and then the Duke said:

"I had no idea that you valued my opinion, but for what it is worth I thought there was no-one to equal you."

Jabina turned round to look at him, her eyes very wide.

"Do you mean that? Do you really mean it?"

"I never say anything I do not mean," the Duke replied quietly.

Then he walked away from her across the Salon to the door of his bed-room.

"Good-night, Jabina," he said in measured tones, and the door closed behind him.

Jabina stood for a moment looking after him.

It was then at that moment she knew that she loved him!

Jabina was late in rising because although her maid brought her a pot of hot chocolate at nine o'clock her eyes were still heavy with sleep.

She sent a message that she would not breakfast with the Duke and rose leisurely, taking time to admire her new gown, which had been delivered, the maid told her, at eight o'clock in the morning.

"The seamstresses have been working all night, M'mselle," the maid said, "and they promised that another evening-gown will be delivered later in the day."

"I cannot believe I could get anything done as quickly in London," Jabina said.

"People are poor in Paris," the maid replied simply, "and orders such as His Grace gave yesterday are a God-send to those who often have few customers. Besides, many who order do not pay."

"Has His Grace paid for these?" Jabina asked.

"Yes, indeed, M'mselle," the maid answered. "His Grace paid for everything as soon as it was delivered. It is much appreciated, I can assure you, M'mselle. Some of the Aristocrats have bills outstanding for years and tradesmen can go bankrupt through having a multitude of debts."

"I have always hated the idea of owing money," Jabina said.

She felt glad that the Duke was as punctilious at paying as he was in other ways.

She had been unable to sleep when she first went to bed for thinking of him.

"Can it really be true?" she asked herself, "that I

have fallen in love with a man who dislikes me and who finds me both irritating and a nuisance?"

She knew now she had felt drawn to him even before the Vicomte had explained the reasons for his solemnity and desire for an obscure and quiet life.

She found herself yearning over him at the thought of his hurt and unhappiness when his mother left him.

She remembered how she had suffered when her own mother had died, and how her father had become more and more dour and unapproachable.

The light had gone out of their house as the light must have gone out at Warminster when the Duchess had run away.

And yet, while she felt for the Duke, she could not help in a way understanding his mother's desire for gaiety, for change, and for love.

It must have been very exciting, Jabina thought, when she had a son who was nearly grown up to be wooed by a man who loved her to such distraction that he was prepared to take her away from England, perhaps to live abroad for the rest of their lives.

She could understand that for an Englishman to leave his country and all that was familiar was perhaps more of a wrench than it was for a woman.

Men's lives were taken up with sport, with the Society of their contemporaries, with their Estates and responsibilities.

Yet Lord Beldon had been prepared to throw all that away for the love of a woman older than himself.

In return the Duchess of Warminster had sacrificed her son.

"How could she do that?" Jabina asked herself.

She could almost feel the anguish that the young Drue had known. It had come like an explosion, as the Vicomte had described it, and that was very understandable.

Children never expected their parents to be almost physically torn and twisted by emotions as they were themselves.

Parents always seemed to be inviolate and free from such distraction.

To Drue, Jabina told herself, it would have been an added shock to realise that his mother was fallible, a woman who would put illicit love before husband, family, and honour.

As usual when Jabina heard or read a story, she lived through the experience of those who were part of it.

Now she could feel the Duchess's indecision as to what steps she should take, and then the desperate moment when she made up her mind.

She could imagine the sense of loss which to her husband must have been intolerable and a physical pain. While Jabina could visualise finally the bewilderment, suffering, and misery of Drue.

'I must help him. I must try to make him happy,' she told herself, and fell asleep thinking of how different and how elegant he had looked in his new clothes.

She was dressed and the maid was arranging her hair in the new fashion when the woman said:

"Will you excuse me, M'mselle, while I fetch you some coffee? It is after ten o'clock and I know both you and His Grace will be ready for it."

"I am indeed!" Jabina said. "And having missed my breakfast I am hungry. Bring me one of those delicious brioches at the same time."

"I will, M'mselle," the maid replied.

She left the room while Jabina put the last finishing touches to her hair and admired the elegant lines of her new gown.

It was of green muslin, extremely simple and designed with a skill which made it, with its green velvet ribbons from Lyon, chic and elegant.

There were frills of lace around the hem and the small puff-sleeves were fashioned entirely of the same lace.

For the daytime it was very transparent, and Jabina could not help wondering what her father and her acquaintances in Scotland would say if they could see her.

She was quite certain they would be deeply shocked!

She was smiling at the thought when she heard the door of her bed-room open.

"You did not take long!" she turned to say to her maid.

Then saw to her surprise that it was the Vicomte who stood there.

"Good-morning . . ." she began.

"Quickly!" he interrupted in an urgent tone. "Bring any money and jewellery you have with you, but nothing else. You are leaving!"

"Leaving?" Jabina echoed. "What do you mean?"

"War has been declared between England and France," he answered, "and Bonaparte has ordered the arrest of all British travellers in the country."

"It cannot be true!" Jabina ejaculated.

"It is true and there are soldiers on their way to take you and Drue to prison."

Through the open door into the Sitting-room Jabina could see the Duke coming from his bed-chamber.

She snatched up a silk shawl she had bought the day before and took the bag containing her mother's jewellery from its hiding-place where she had put it the night before on the top of her wardrobe.

"Hurry! Hurry!" the Vicomte was saying. "They will be here at any moment."

Jabina ran into the Salon.

The Duke was standing in the centre of the room and without thinking, because she needed his protection, she slipped her hand into his.

"It is all right," he said in a steady voice. "Armand will save us."

"I only hope I can do so," the Vicomte said. "Follow me!"

He went from the Salon and Jabina and the Duke followed him.

To her surprise they did not go downstairs but climbed up the staircase to the first, second, third, and fourth floors.

Now they were in the attics and the Vicomte opened

a door at the far end of a small dusty room which could not have been used for a long time.

It was filled with ancient trunks, broken china, and chairs that had lost an arm or a leg.

It was lit only by a sky-light and Jabina saw a ladder against one of the walls.

The Vicomte and the Duke adjusted it into position and locked the door behind them.

"They will search the rest of the house first," the Vicomte said, "but I was only a few minutes ahead of them. In fact I saw them marching in this direction as I came to collect you in my carriage."

"They must not connect you with our disappearance," the Duke said.

"I can look after myself," the Vicomte answered. "Come on, Drue. Let us hope Jabina is as agile as you used to be in climbing over the roofs of Paris."

Jabina wondered why the Duke had climbed them in the past, but there was no time to ask questions.

The two men hurried her up the ladder and she found herself standing in a deep gully between the high, grey, gabled roofs which rose on either side of it.

The Vicomte drew the ladder up beside them and laid it down on the roof. Then he secured the sky-light.

They then followed his lead, walking along in gullies, climbing up small narrow ladders to roofs which were higher than the one they were on, and then down ladders on the other side.

At times there was a dangerous and terrifying drop into the street below.

It seemed to Jabina that they walked for miles. The skirt of her pretty new gown was soon black with dust and dirt, and so were her hands.

She found the bag in which she carried her mother's jewellery an encumbrance, and the Duke, taking it from her, managed to insert it into an inside pocket of his coat where it bulged, but no-one at the moment was thinking about appearances.

By the time Jabina thought they must have walked

half-way across Paris, they came to another sky-light similar to the one they had used to reach the roofs, and climbed down into yet another attic room.

The house in which they now found themselves was very different from the one they had left. It appeared to be empty and the windows were boarded up. The floors were thick with dust and rats scuttled away at their approach.

They went down staircases of which the balustrades were broken and the foot-boards had holes in them.

They reached the ground floor and Jabina thought they must be going out into the street. But instead the Vicomte crossed the Hall.

Behind the main staircase there was a narrow, even more precarious one, which must once have been used by servants.

They went down this, and passing through what appeared to be a heavy cellar door they found themselves in a huge Cavern which to Jabina's astonishment was filled with people.

There were more men than women but they were not, as might have been expected, people of lower class, but all of them were elegantly dressed and apparently Aristocrats.

They were certainly not sitting doing nothing. Each of them seemed to be engaged in some task or another. The men had papers, probably maps, in front of them and the women were sorting out clothes.

At the far end of the Cavern a very distinguished-looking elderly man with grey hair was sitting behind a trestle-table, and the Vicomte led Jabina and the Duke up to him.

"May I introduce His Grace the Duke of Warminster, *Monsieur,*" he said, "and his sister, Lady Jabina Minster."

The older man rose and held out his hand.

"I am the Duc de St. Croix," he said. "I am delighted that Armand could rescue you in time."

"You must forgive me if I seem a little bewildered by what is happening," the Duke said.

"As Armand will have told you," the Duc de St. Croix answered, "the Corsican has ordered your arrest."

"Why?" the Duke asked. "When war is declared it is not usual for the authorities to proceed immediately against civilians."

"What can you expect from an untamed barbarian?" the Duc de St. Croix enquired, almost spitting out the words.

"What has infuriated Bonaparte," the Vicomte explained, "is that two French brigs have been captured at sea by British ships. From this moment the Continent is closed to the British and those that are already here are to be treated as prisoners of war."

"It is incredible!" the Duke ejaculated.

"That is what we think," the Duc de St. Croix agreed. "But nothing surprises us where Bonaparte is concerned."

The Vicomte smiled.

"It would be a feather in his cap to have the Duke of Warminster as his prisoner. God knows how long the war will last!"

"It will last until the British beat Napoleon's Army," the Duc de St. Croix said briefly. "Now, Your Grace, we have to decide in what disguise it would be best for you to leave Paris."

"Have you sent to the Employment Exchange?" the Vicomte asked.

"One of our best men set out over an hour ago to obtain information," the Duc replied. "He should not be long now."

He looked at the Duke.

"How good is your French?"

"Very good—for an Englishman!" the Vicomte answered for him. "But not good enough for a Frenchman!"

"You will have to come from one of the Northern Provinces," The Duc de St. Croix said. "And *M'mselle?*"

"Perfect!" the Vicomte said before Jabina could speak.

Jabina was just about to say that her mother had been half French when she remembered that she was supposed to be the Duke's sister and bit back the words with an effort.

As if he was aware she had nearly made a slip, the Duke looked at her with a smile and she smiled back at him.

She had the feeling that he was rather excited by what was happening, while on the other hand she was very apprehensive.

She had heard tales of the savagery of the French, the vengefulness they had exhibited in the countries they had conquered, and their callous indifference to the sufferings of the ordinary people.

She was sure that if she and the Duke were taken to prison they would be separated from each other, and she was terrified at the thought of being shut away alone.

It was horrifying!

Once again she slipped her hand into the Duke's and felt the warm strength of his fingers. It was very comforting.

"What I am thinking might be best for you . . ." the Duc de St. Croix had begun when suddenly the door at the far end of the Cavern opened and everyone turned towards it.

A thin, middle-aged man came in looking, Jabina thought, rather like a superior clerk or perhaps a secretary to a Nobleman.

He was dressed in black and there was something about his whole appearance and the way in which he moved that made her sure that anything he undertook he would carry out precisely and intelligently, with attention to every detail.

He walked up to the trestle-table at which the Duc de St. Croix was seated, who said quickly:

"Any news, Mirmon?"

"Yes indeed, *Monsieur le Duc,*" the man answered. "The Marquis of Lorne has left for Switzerland disguised as a chambermaid employed by the wife of a

Swiss Banker. There should be no difficulty in getting him over the Frontier."

"That is excellent!" the Duc de St. Croix said. "And there are vacancies at the Bureau?"

"Yes, *Monsieur le Duc,* and one in particular which should fit the lady and gentleman you have in mind."

"What is it?" the Duc asked.

"General Delmas has been appointed Commander at Le Havre. He wishes to leave Paris tomorrow morning."

It seemed to Jabina that everyone was listening breathlessly to the quiet voice.

"Yes?"

"He and Madame Delmas are unable to take with them their own valet and *femme de chambre*. Those in their service have several children. They have therefore requested two persons suitable for such employment to be furnished for them immediately."

"Excellent!" the Duc de St. Croix said. "Armand, ask the Comte to prepare the papers. The Duke will have been invalided out of the Army and he can have been born in Normandy. That will account for his somewhat Anglicised accent. *M'mselle* can be from Lyon or anywhere within a reasonable radius of Paris."

The Vicomte left the trestle-table to walk across the Cavern to where at another table a gentleman was obviously dealing with papers and travel documents.

"Excuse me, *Monsieur le Duc,*" the man called Mirmon said.

"Yes, what is it?" the Duc enquired.

"The General has asked for a married couple. It would be best for the lady and gentleman to be married."

"Yes, yes of course," the Duc agreed. "There will be no difficulty in that, I suppose?"

"No difficulty," the Duke answered.

Jabina held out her hand.

"My mother's wedding-ring is with the other jewellery," she said to him in a low voice.

He looked down at her and she saw there was a

faint smile on his face. She knew they were both thinking the same thing.

It was impossible for them to escape each other. Fate, circumstance, call it what you will, threw them together irrevocably as husband and wife!

Then as the Duke took the little bag from his pocket and placed it in her hands their fingers touched.

It was only by accident—only the faintest brush—and yet Jabina felt a sudden thrill run through her, a sensation such as she had never known before.

It was almost like a flame.

'I love him!' she thought to herself. 'Whatever happens to us, it does not matter as long as we are together!'

Chapter Six

Seated on the box of the travelling carriage, Jabina realised with interest that one could see so much better than if one was a passenger inside.

They had set off from the General's house at eight o'clock in the morning, and she felt as if she had already done several hours' work before the trunks had finally been strapped and carried downstairs.

A multitude of small packages of articles which had been forgotten had been bundled into baskets and bags at the last moment and stowed away somewhere in the coach.

It certainly looked an impressive vehicle and one which could achieve the speed the General required of it.

From the moment Jabina and the Duke had met the General they had realised that he behaved like a despot accustomed to getting his own way in the shortest possible time.

Armed by the Royalists with their papers, they had walked from the narrow dirty street where the Cavern was situated to the better part of Paris where they were to present themselves for employment.

If Jabina had not been so frightened at the thought of what would happen if they were exposed, she would have found their appearance amusing.

In the Cavern she had undressed behind a screen and the ladies had redressed her in the clothes befitting a *femme de chambre*.

They were insistent that every detail should be correct.

The close-fitting black-serge dress would have been ugly on anyone who had not such a perfect figure as Jabina's. A white collar and small silk apron relieved its severity. A dark, coarse straw bonnet covered her hair.

Her hair had given them quite a problem.

"The red is too alluring!" declared one of the ladies who was addressed by the others as "Comtesse," and there was a touch of envy in her voice.

"That is true!" another agreed. "No good Housekeeper would engage you if there were men in the house."

They all laughed, but Jabina said anxiously:

"I suppose I could dye my hair?"

"There is no time," the Comtesse replied. "Besides, dyed hair always looks un-natural."

Eventually after some discussion they had dragged Jabina's hair back from her forehead and arranged it in a bun on top of her head.

They then dusted it with a dark powder which dulled the brilliance of the colour and left her looking definitely more subdued.

"Her skin is too white for a French woman!" the Comtesse complained and again Jabina thought her voice was envious.

The others said this was ridiculous.

"Josephine Bonaparte has a white skin," they said. "The English are not the only people in the world with fair complexions!"

It was then decided to concentrate on Jabina's attire and hope that the General's wife, in her hurry to get to Le Havre with her husband, would not notice her too closely.

Her shift was of thick calico which was rough and tough. Her stockings were of black wool, and they had some difficulty in finding a suitable pair of shoes which were both sensible and small enough.

Finally the rest of the clothes she would have to wear were put into a wicker basket which the ladies told her could be bought for a franc or so at any cheap shop in Paris.

There was a cotton dress to wear when she was working; a white mob-cap which would at least cover her hair, and a highly starched white apron.

"Do not forget it is your employer who provides your uniform," the Comtesse said, "so Madame Delmas will not be surprised that you have so few things."

Finally they provided Jabina with a travelling-cloak which had obviously seen a lot of wear.

"It belongs to my own *femme de chambre*," one of the ladies said with a smile, "and here also are her gloves."

"Did she not wonder why you wanted them?" a lady asked.

"I told her it was for *les pauvres*. The nuns are always collecting for the poor of Paris, and of course I offered her replacements—things that I had worn myself which she would obviously prefer."

The ladies laughed.

When Jabina was ready she came from behind the screen, having taken a last somewhat wistful look at her new green muslin gown which she had worn for the first and last time.

She felt a little shy at seeing the Duke and wondered what he would think of her appearance. But when she saw him, she knew she need endure no criticism from him.

He certainly looked extraordinary.

He was wearing the normal tight black breeches and closely buttoned coat of a Frenchman in service, but he also sported a patch over one eye.

As Jabina looked at him in astonishment the Duke said with a smile:

"Armand thinks this is a very effective disguise. He does not believe that anyone would deliberately blind themselves."

He laughed.

"Also the wound on the head that I received when we first met is now proving useful."

Although in the last few days the wound had been mending fast, it now, Jabina saw, had been made to look far worse again.

The bruising round it had almost vanished, but there were still scabs where the Doctor had sewed the cut with six stitches and which now seemed to blaze out on the Duke's forehead above the patch over his eye.

There was no doubt that anyone seeing him would assume he had been wounded in battle.

"Do not forget," the Comte said as he prepared the papers, "that you have been discharged from the Army also owing to a bullet wound in your leg. Remember to limp slightly and not move too quickly."

"I will do that," the Duke said.

He picked up the papers that were handed to him and placed them in an inside pocket.

"Your names are Jacques and Maria Boucher," the Comte continued.

"One thing has been forgotten," the Duc de St. Croix interposed, "and a very important one."

"What is that?" the Duke enquired.

"Your hands," the older man replied. "A number of Aristocrats were captured during the Revolution simply because they forgot to disguise their hands."

"Of course! I should have thought of it!" one of the ladies cried.

Producing a pair of nail-scissors, she took the Duke's hand in hers and cut his nails very short.

"Now scratch your hands on the ground," the Duc de St. Croix added. "That is an effective way of making them look rough and as if occasionally you did a little work!"

They all laughed, but Jabina knew that everything they said was in fact very serious.

The Vicomte looked at his watch.

"If you are ready," he said, "I think you should be going to your interview with the General. It would be a mistake to let another couple get engaged ahead of you."

"Yes, of course," the Duke answered.

He held out his hand to the Duc de St. Croix.

"May I thank Your Grace for your kindness and help."

"We do not need thanks," the Duc said, "but if you can at any time, when you reach England, assist the Royalist Cause, we should be more than grateful."

"You know I will do anything that is in my power," the Duke answered.

The Duc looked at the Comte.

"You have given His Grace the names of our Royalist agents in case they should be discovered before they reach Le Havre?"

"I have," the Comte replied.

"You realise, I am sure, that you must turn to them for help only in an emergency?" the Duc said. "Every contact that is made with them by someone like yourselves exposes them to danger."

"I am well aware of that," the Duke answered.

"And another thing," the Duc went on, "your only chance of getting back to England is, as you know, to contact the smugglers who will be crossing the Channel every night now that war has been declared."

He smiled.

"Bonaparte, of course, as he did before, will give them every possible facility because when they reach these shores they will bring him gold. But they will certainly not be allowed to carry passengers on the return journey!"

"I realise that," the Duke said.

"Therefore I suspect," the Duc went on, "there will be sentries on guard along the Coastline. That may be one of the reasons for sending more troops to Le Havre, Calais, and Boulogne."

He paused and added:

"Of course Bonaparte may be preparing to put into operation immediately his ambition of invading England."

"He will never be able to do that!" the Duke retorted.

"That is what we think," the Duc agreed, "but at the same time he may attempt it."

"Whether he does or not," the Vicomte interposed, "there will be a number of troops guarding the Coast. So be very careful how you approach the creeks or bays where the smugglers will be bringing in their boats."

"I will!" the Duke said, "and thank you, Armand. One day I may be able to repay you."

"One day," the Vicomte said, "I shall be happy when you and Lady Jabina will be able to spend more time in Paris."

"I was so looking forward to visiting the Dance-Garden again," Jabina said in a wistful voice, "and I have never seen the Louvre."

He lifted her hand to his lips, and then as the Duke turned aside to say good-bye to the Duc de St. Croix he said in a low voice that only she could hear:

"This is your chance to help Drue—you realise that?"

"You know that I will try to make him happy," Jabina answered, and once again the Vicomte kissed her hand.

There was no time to say more.

They were taken to the front of the house to climb alone up the dirty, broken, basements steps to the pavement.

They walked quickly and spoke little.

"From now on we must converse with each other only in French," the Duke said in a low voice. "Not only will it be dangerous to speak English, but it might also improve my accent!"

"Try to make your voice sound a little common," Jabina advised.

Then she taught him some of the idioms which a servant in his position would be most likely to use.

The General was younger than Jabina had expected, until she remembered that Bonaparte regularly promoted young men to high rank in the Army.

He had a long nose and eyes that seemed uncomfortably penetrating.

"In what Regiment were you? Where were you wounded?" he asked the Duke, firing question after question at him in quick succession.

Fortunately the Duke had already been given every detail of his supposed Army career.

He answered servilely, clipping his words and slurring some of his vowels, which made his French sound less Anglicised and far more convincing.

"You come from Normandy, I see," the General remarked, looking at his papers. "Is your family still there?"

"*Oui, Mon Général,*" the Duke replied. "That's one of the reasons why my wife and I would like to come with you and Madame to Le Havre."

"I shall expect you to work hard," the General said sharply. "Are you fit enough to take employment?"

"The Doctors say so, *Mon Général.*"

The General turned his attention to Jabina.

"You have been in service before, Maria?" he asked.

Jabina, who had also been given a reference, explained that she had been a lady's-maid for two years to a Lady of Fashion who had unfortunately left Paris for her country Estate.

"There was no place for my husband in her household, Monsieur, so I stayed behind and we hope to find employment where we can be together."

"Yes, yes. I understand," the General said. "Well, Madame Delmas will instruct you in your duties, and if you stay here tonight you can help our servants with the packing and find out from them the way we both like things done."

"We are engaged, *Mon Général?*" the Duke enquired.

"You are engaged," the General said briefly, "but if you are not satisfactory I shall dismiss you both when we reach Le Havre."

"I hope we shall prove satisfactory," the Duke said humbly.

There was so much to do that Jabina, who had wondered what sleeping arrangements would be made for them, found that she was expected to snatch no more than an hour's sleep on a sofa before she was awakened to finish the packing and help Madame Delmas to dress for the journey.

The General's wife was not a particularly attractive woman, a few years older than her husband.

Jabina soon discovered that she gave herself airs because she was better bred than the General and had made, according to her family, quite a *mésalliance* by marrying a man whose career lay only in the Army.

"She has the money!" her employer's lady's-maid hissed in Jabina's ear.

Jabina felt that that must have been the reason for the General's choice.

Despite his sharpness and the way he ordered everyone about as if they were troops under his command, Jabina felt that of the two he was the nicer.

But she was not particularly concerned with the characters or personalities of her employers.

All she wished to do was to get out of Paris, feeling quite certain that Napoleon's soldiers would be searching for them, having not found them as had been expected in their Apartment.

The coach drawn by four horses moved off slowly and soon joined the other coaches, chaises, and *cabriolets* which drove with amazing rapidity over the irregular paving-stones of Paris.

From inside the carriage yesterday, Jabina had not noticed what a deafening noise the traffic made splashing through the gutters which ran down the middle of the streets.

She had also not been aware that the lack of foot-pavements such as there were in London made it very dangerous for those who had to walk.

She thought that the poor pedestrians hurrying to work, shopping, or going inoffensively about their business were driven about by the coaches and *cabriolets* like a flock of frightened sheep.

She saw in the short space between the General's house and the gates of Paris quite a number of accidents, and the dirt and water from the roads being spattered over clean skirts and gentlemen's stockings until she felt thankful that she was being driven behind the horses.

Once through the gates of Paris they began to move at a speed which Jabina thought must equal the *diligence*'s.

The coachman confirmed this idea when he told the Duke that the General wished to reach Verdon before nightfall, which was eighty-one miles away.

"Can we really manage that?" the Duke enquired.

"Certainly," the coachman replied. "We shall change horses every twelve to fifteen miles, and soldiers have already been sent ahead to reserve the best animals for the General."

It was however difficult to have much conversation.

Jabina was concerned with keeping her seat and not falling from the box of the coach when they sped round a corner or were drawn unexpectedly to a halt by being held up or meeting another vehicle.

As if the Duke realised her predicament, he put his arm round her waist and drew her closer to him.

"I should have let you sit on the inside," he said quietly. "You would be safer that way, but I thought you would dislike being squeezed between the coachman and myself."

She knew he had been thinking of her and knowing that she would be disgusted by the close proximity of a coachman who smelt of garlic and sweat, but who was however quite proficient with the reins.

"I will be all right," Jabina answered.

She was very conscious of the strength of the Duke's arm and the fact that he was so close to her that neither of them could move without the other being aware of it.

Nevertheless the Duke insisted on their changing places when they reached the first Posting-Inn.

Here Madame Delmas, while she did not alight, demanded coffee and the General a glass of wine.

The Duke had to scramble agilely down from the coach to fetch it for them from the Inn. Then almost before he had time to hand back the china and the glass they had used, the coachman was whipping up the fresh horses.

"Here—not so fast, friend!" the Duke pleaded. "Remember I have had a bullet in my leg and it slows me up."

"Sorry, Comrade," the coachman replied, "but the General's in a hurry to get to grips with the English. If I don't get the speed out of these mule-like creatures, like as not he'll blow my head off!"

"A harsh man, is he?" the Duke enquired.

"Those as serve under him say he can be the very devil if he chooses."

Jabina felt herself shiver apprehensively.

The Duke, thinking she was cold, drew her cloak more closely round her.

"I must try to find you a rug," he said in a considerate voice that made her feel that he cared a little for her well-being.

"I am not cold," she answered.

"We can at least be thankful it is not raining," the Duke smiled.

The day seemed endless.

They stopped at noon for a quick meal. The Duke and Jabina were expected to eat in the kitchen of the Inn, which Jabina at any rate found amusing.

There were strings of onions hanging on the wall, brass pots and pans, ham smoking up in the rafters.

It was all quite picturesque, but it certainly did not compensate for the dirt on the floor and the slovenly manner in which the cooking was done.

Strangely enough what they ate tasted good, but there was no doubt that an English cook would have been horrified at the dirt and debris.

Whenever they stopped at Posting-Inns in the country villages, there were always a number of beggars to ask for alms from the General and his wife, and also soldiers who had lost legs or arms and who appeared to be almost in rags.

"Is nothing done for them once they have been discharged from the Army?" Jabina asked the Duke.

"Does any country worry about the men who fight for it once they are no longer of any use?" the Duke replied almost savagely.

Jabina was so tired by the time the afternoon came that her head began to nod, and the Duke pulled her a little closer to him and she slept against his shoulder.

She had had little sleep the night before, and the unusual exertion of bending over trunks, running up and down many flights of stairs, and being at the beck and call of Madame Delmas's querulous voice made her feel more tired than she had ever been before.

When her eyes closed she was conscious that they were still moving.

She could hear the crack of the whip, the sound of the wheels moving over rough roads; but it sometimes seemed far away and was mixed with her dreams.

It was with a start that she heard the Duke say:

"We are there," and awakened to find they were driving into the yard of a large, quite impressive-looking Inn.

"Are we at Verdon?" she enquired.

"Eighty-one miles in just over seven hours!" the coachman said with satisfaction.

At any time when she was travelling Jabina would have welcomed the idea of a rest from the movement of the coach and something to eat.

Now she had her duties to perform first.

Madame Delmas was escorted up to the best bed-chamber in the Inn.

She required particular trunks from the coach, all of which seemed to be at the bottom of the pile stacked on the roof.

There was also hot water to be fetched; her gown

to be changed; her hair to be re-arranged; and all the time Jabina was attending to her, she complained that they were travelling too fast and that it was insensitive of the General to expect it of her.

"Who wants," she asked, not once but a dozen times, "to be isolated in a place like Le Havre when I might be in Paris?"

As she was obviously expected to answer, Jabina said tentatively:

"I am sure, Madame, that the General's appointment is of the utmost importance."

"Of course it is!" Madame Delmas snapped. "But I am not a soldier and too much, I tell you, is expected of a soldier's wife!"

She paused to ask:

"I suppose your husband can look after the General properly? We cannot be bothered by having sick people on our hands."

"No indeed, Madame," Jabina replied. "My husband will be quite capable of fulfilling his duties."

"So I should hope!" Madame Delmas snorted.

Finally, when she was ready to descend to the private parlour for supper, she gave Jabina a long list of things she required for the night.

They included a change of pillows, more blankets, and a bed-warmer to be placed between the sheets for at least an hour before she retired.

To be sure she would not forget what had been ordered, Jabina went in search of the Inn-keeper or his wife.

She thought she had seen very little of them since their arrival and realised the reason was that the Posting-Inn was packed with soldiers.

She could hear them talking and laughing in the Tavern, which was the public part of the Inn, and she could also hear female voices mingling with theirs.

She found the Inn-keeper's wife in the kitchen busy cooking the supper.

"More blankets? Fresh pillows?" the woman exclaimed. "We have none! The Inn is full, every room is occupied. You will have to take them off your own bed, or she can go without."

Jabina saw no reason why she should be cold to suit Madame Delmas.

She therefore found the Duke and suggested that he bring in one of the thick, fur-lined carriage-rugs.

He brought one from the coach and carried it upstairs to Madame Delmas's room.

"Have you had anything to eat?" he asked Jabina after he had put the rug on the bed.

"I have not had a moment to breathe!" Jabina answered. "But since you mention it, I am hungry!"

"Come along," he said. "Before you do anything else, you must be fed."

"Was the General difficult?" Jabina enquired.

"A trifle impatient," the Duke said with a smile. "I shall always have the greatest respect in the future for my valet's quickness. I never knew how difficult it was to remove Army boots. Especially for a man who is inclined to kick you while you do it!"

Jabina found herself laughing helplessly.

Then they went downstairs and literally helped themselves to food in the kitchen while the Inn-keeper's wife grumbled at them, and the Inn-keeper, who was hurrying in and out with trays and bottles, pushed them out of the way.

Finally they took their plates and sitting on an oak settle in the passage ate more or less in comfort.

"This is really an adventure!" Jabina said.

"I am glad you look at it like that," the Duke answered. "I have been thanking our lucky stars for Armand ever since we left Paris."

Jabina gave a little shudder.

"I too," she said in a low voice, "have thought how frightening it would be to be shut up in a French prison, especially if they would not let me be with you."

"It might have been possible if I convinced them

that you were my wife, but it would have required a lot of explaining why I introduced you to Paris as my sister."

"My nurse always used to say 'one lie leads to another,' " Jabina said.

"I am sure that is true," the Duke agreed, "at the same time I am praying that our disguise, if you count it as a lie, will be successful."

"How much longer do we have to stay with them?" Jabina asked.

"Until we reach Quillebeuf, where I understand we are staying tomorrow night," the Duke replied. "It is about thirty-five miles from Le Havre and it lies near the sea. What we will have to decide is when to make for the Coast—before we reach Le Havre, where there is a very strong garrison of soldiers, or try our luck at Quillebeuf when our employers are asleep."

"I think it would be wise to wait and see what it looks like," Jabina replied.

The Duke smiled.

"Strangely enough that is what I have decided myself."

The Landlord passed them and Jabina called out:

"*Monsieur,* have the General and Madame finished their dinner?"

"They have," he replied, "and Madame is talking of retiring to bed."

"Then I must go and see to her," Jabina said quickly.

"I will wait for you on the stairs," the Duke said. "I have carried up your luggage. We are sleeping in the attic."

"I might have guessed that!" Jabina grinned and then she hurried away to attend to Madame Delmas.

It took her some time. In fact it was nearly two hours later when Madame finally got into bed and, while complaining about having to sleep under the carriage-rug, accepted there was no alternative.

Jabina had to pin up Madame's hair in neat curls after brushing it for over one hundred strokes.

She required to have her feet massaged with a special lotion, her hands with another, and her back with yet a third.

There seemed to be no end to the different beauty preparations with which Madame Delmas attempted to enhance her looks.

The result, Jabina could not help thinking, was not very satisfactory.

After she had made up the fire, tidied away Madame's clothes, and seen that the window was securely shut, she was permitted to blow out the candles and leave her employer in the darkness.

She was not surprised to find that the Duke was no longer on the stairs and thought he might be waiting where they had eaten their dinner.

She went down to the ground floor and now she heard music very like the gay, compelling sounds to which she had danced last night coming from the Tavern.

They were dancing!

Jabina felt that her feet itched to dance too.

She was no longer tired.

She felt some of the excitement that had been hers the night before flow over her as she listened to the exhilarating sounds. It meant, she felt, that soldiers were twirling round in a waltz such as she had danced in the Duke's arms.

Impulsively and without thinking it might be an unwise thing to do, she put out her hand to open the door which led into the Tavern.

Even as she did so she heard the Duke's voice say:

"Jabina!"

She turned to see him coming down the corridor.

"Where are you going?" he asked.

"They are dancing," she said, her eyes shining. "Oh, Drue, let us join them!"

"Are you crazy?" he asked. "You cannot go in there."

"Why not?" she enquired.

"Because it would be a mistake."

"Oh, do not be so stuffy! Nobody will take any notice of us. I know there are soldiers but I expect the local people come in from the village as well."

"It is time you went to bed," the Duke said. "We have to be up early in the morning."

"I want to dance," Jabina said. "Just one dance."

"No!"

The Duke's voice was uncompromising.

"Well you can do as you like," Jabina cried. "I am going in . . . not to dance but to watch the others."

Once again she put her hand towards the door.

Then to her surprise the Duke took hold of her arm and pulling her away took her forcibly towards another narrow staircase which led, Jabina guessed, to the cheaper rooms in the Inn.

"You are going to bed!" the Duke said sternly.

Because his voice was so authoritative she felt annoyed.

"You have no right to order me about," she said, "and quite frankly I can see no danger in joining in the dancing for a few minutes. If we were really what we pretend to be, that is exactly what we could do."

"You are going to bed," the Duke said firmly.

"As usual you are making everything dull and depressing," Jabina flashed at him. "Why can you not enjoy yourself for a change?"

They were half-way up the staircase by now and it was clear that it ran along the side of the Tavern, the noise from the musicians and the dancers being almost deafening.

On the side of the staircase a little lower than eye level there was a small glass window, little more than a peep-hole, which was undoubtedly used at times by the Landlord if he wished to keep an eye on his guests without being observed.

The Duke took a quick glance through it and pulling Jabina by the arm drew her nearer.

"Is that the sort of thing in which you wish to take part?" he asked harshly.

Jabina looked through the window.

The Tavern, as she had expected, had a long bar on one side of it, where the Landlord was filling glasses and tankards of beer.

There were two musicians, one playing an accordion, the other a violin, and making a surprising amount of noise.

There were two or three soldiers dancing, but they were quite obviously drunk and were dragging their partners around the floor in a manner which made it seem surprising that they could even keep on their feet.

At tables round the room soldiers were sitting with their arms round women who were attired in a tawdry manner such as Jabina had never seen before, their faces painted to match the flamboyant feathers in their hats.

A number of them were unclothed to the waist. The rest were displaying their legs in a manner which seemed to Jabina to be shockingly indecent.

One woman was screaming half with laughter, half with fear, as two soldiers lifted her onto a table.

In corners of the room women and soldiers were lying embraced on the floor.

Jabina gave a little gasp. She hardly had time to take in what she saw before the Duke drew her away.

"Do you still want to dance?" he asked angrily.

"I . . . I did not . . know it would be . . . . like that."

"Another time you might trust me to know what is best," the Duke said coldly.

They reached the top of the stairs, where there was one cheap taper set in a candlestick to light a landing on which there were four doors.

The Duke opened the one nearest and taking up the candle carried it into the room.

It was, Jabina saw, an attic bed-room, the whole room dominated by a large bed piled with mattresses in French fashion, which made it very high.

There was practically no other furniture in the room except one hard chair and a china basin with a ewer beside it standing on the floor.

"Not very prepossessing!" the Duke said dryly.

He turned from his contemplation of the room to look at Jabina as he spoke and saw that her eyes were still wide and frightened from what she had seen happening in the Tavern.

"It is all right, Jabina," he said kindly. "Lock your door. You will be quite safe here."

"Where are . . . you going to . . . sleep?"

"I will find somewhere," he replied.

"But the Inn-keeper's wife said the Inn was full . . . there will be people coming up to sleep in the other rooms . . . you cannot leave me . . . alone."

"I have already suggested that you lock the door."

He held the candle higher as he spoke. Both he and Jabina saw that the door, made in the cheapest possible way, had only a latch. There was no bolt and no lock and key.

"Please do . . . not . . . leave me."

"Very well," the Duke answered. "You get into bed and I will sleep on the chair."

"That is ridiculous!" Jabina exclaimed. "You need your sleep as much as I do. We can both sleep in the bed. It is quite large enough."

It was true it was a large bed, but for a moment the Duke was very still.

Then he said in a matter-of-fact voice:

"Of course, we will do that."

"Why not?" Jabina asked. "After all no-one will know, and we are married . . . really married."

"Yes, we are married," the Duke repeated. "Get into bed, Jabina. I will wait outside until you are undressed."

The manner in which he walked from the room seemed to her abrupt and impolite and she thought with a sudden feeling of despair that he must dislike the necessity of being so near to her.

'He hates me!' she told herself. 'I have been nothing but an encumbrance and a nuisance to him ever since we met.'

It was however not a moment for introspection.

Jabina took off the ugly clothes in which the Aristocrats had dressed her and found in her wicker basket a night-gown made of coarse cotton which fastened at the neck.

She washed in cold water, then climbed into bed.

She seemed to be as far from the floor as the box of the coach had seemed above ground level.

There were several mattresses, one on top of the other, and on top of that one of feathers into which Jabina sank.

She pulled the coarse cotton sheets and the blankets up to her chin and called out:

"Drue!"

She thought for a moment that he had left her, and then the door opened and he came in.

"It is quite comfortable," she said, "and I have pushed the feathers to make a little mountain between us. I will not make you uncomfortable. We could almost be in two different continents."

"That is undoubtedly re-assuring," he remarked and she was not certain if he was laughing at her or not.

She had placed her clothes in a neat pile on top of her wicker basket.

The Duke took off his coat and put it over the back of the only chair.

Then he leant forward and blew out the taper.

He undressed in silence and Jabina felt the bed heave as he climbed into it.

She could feel the feathers fluff out like a balloon making a complete barrier between them.

"Are you all right?" she asked.

"Perfectly," he answered. "This is certainly more comfortable than where I spent last night."

"Where was that?" Jabina asked.

"On top of a bed I shared with one of the flunkies," he answered. "We decided there was not time to undress so we lay down as we were."

Jabina laughed.

"I am sure His Grace the Duke of Warminster never

realised before what uncomfortable lives servants lead!"

"I shall certainly be more sympathetic to my staff in future," the Duke said.

"Will we . . . reach England?" Jabina asked.

"We have done quite well so far," the Duke answered. "The General speaks to me as one soldier to another. I am quite certain he is not in the least suspicious."

"Madame speaks to me as if I were a slave."

There was silence for they were both tired. Then when the Duke felt he was floating away into oblivion Jabina said:

"Drue!"

"What is it?"

"When two people sleep . . . together in a bed they have a . . . baby . . . you do not . . . think that we . . ."

"No!" the Duke said decisively.

There was a silence and after a moment she said:

"I expect . . . they do something more than just . . . sleep beside one another. I have often . . . wondered what it was, but . . . there was no-one to . . . ask."

Again there was silence and she went on hesitatingly:

"As we are . . . sort of . . . married, you would not like to . . . tell me?"

"Another time," the Duke said. "You should go to sleep now. You have a long day ahead of you."

He thought she must have obeyed him, but after a long pause she said again:

"Is it . . . nice what two people do . . . together?"

"Very nice—if they love each other," the Duke replied.

"But you . . . do not . . . love me . . . ?" Jabina murmured, her voice trailing away into silence.

After a while the Duke knew by her quiet breathing that she was asleep.

He turned over very carefully so as not to disturb her.

But he did not sleep for a long time.

Chapter Seven

They arrived at Quillebeuf late in the following afternoon. It had on the whole been an easy journey
despite the twisting road over the last part of the route.

Quillebeuf, which stood on the Seine, was a small
rather attractive little hamlet with one good Inn.

It seemed a strange place for the General to wish to
stop until Jabina remembered that it would only take
him under four hours to reach Le Havre the next day,
when he could arrive early in the afternoon to be
greeted with due ceremony.

It had become very warm in the day and she had
found the sun on her face and neck very tiring as they
drove at the usual break-neck speed required by the
General.

The coachman had been pushing his horses with
what Jabina thought almost amounted to cruelty.

As on the previous day it was almost impossible to
make conversation, and she therefore contented herself by sitting close to the Duke and wondering if
he thought of her as much as she thought of him.

He had awakened her from a deep sleep at six in
the morning, and for a moment she found it hard to
realise where she was.

The big cumbersome bed had been very comfortable
and she had hardly moved all night.

The Duke was already up and dressed and the room
was alight with the sun coming in through the uncur-
tained windows.

"Madame will be requiring her coffee in another hour," the Duke said. "You had best get dressed and go downstairs for something to eat—otherwise you may miss your breakfast."

Sleepily Jabina had smiled up at him, her red hair loose over the pillows, her eyes still dreamy with sleep.

He looked very strange, she thought, with the patch already over his eye, his wound red on his forehead.

"I was . . . dreaming," she said drowsily.

He looked down at her and for a moment she thought there was an expression of kindness in his eyes.

Then he turned away.

"Hurry, Jabina!" he said. "We do not wish to give our employers reason for being angry with us, and it is vital for us to reach Quillebeuf."

He went from the room shutting the door behind him, and she heard his footsteps going down the uncarpeted stairs.

It seemed strange, she thought, to know that they had slept side by side last night, and yet there was the balloon of feathers still high in the bed and, as she had said to the Duke, they might just as well have been in two different continents.

She wondered what he would have said if she had moved across the bed into his arms and said:

"I love you!"

In her imagination she could feel him stiffen and say that he did not love her and wished only to be free!

'Why did I have to meet him?' Jabina asked despairingly.

Then she knew that even if the Duke did not love her, and that when she must leave him they might never meet again, yet he would always be in her heart.

"I love him . . . I love him . . ." she said aloud.

But she must not annoy him by being late in attending to Madame Delmas.

Jabina dressed quickly. Then packing her nightgown away in her wicker basket, she carried it downstairs.

She fancied she would have little time to climb again

to the attic once the General decided he wished to be on his way.

She was right in her assumption.

She had hardly finished dressing Madame Delmas before there were a number of messages telling her the General was waiting and the coach was at the door.

Sitting on the box-seat, Jabina felt she ought to be looking at the countryside, taking an interest in the peasants in the fields and the small hamlets through which they passed.

The Seine meandered on the right of them, the silvery water appearing always to be in view however twisting the road.

But instead Jabina found herself thinking of the Duke.

So much seemed to have happened so quickly that her recollections of everything that had occurred had become jumbled in her mind.

She found herself remembering his appearance when she had walked into the Salon to find his sombre garments had been discarded and instead he was a 'Beau' in the real sense of the word.

She thought how much fun it had been when they had danced together in the garden to the gay music of the noisy, bourgeois band.

Most of all she found herself thinking of what the Vicomte had told her and wondering if this strange adventure in which they were taking part together would propel the Duke out of the dull austerity into which he had fashioned his life.

'He is no longer dull where I am concerned. I love him,' Jabina told herself.

Whatever he was like she still wanted to be with him.

It was difficult sitting close beside him not to let him know that she thrilled to the strength of his arm round her waist and from the nearness of his shoulder.

She had slept against him yesterday afternoon, but then she had rested her head unconsciously. Now she longed to rub her cheek against him; to look up into his eyes and tell him of her love.

She pulled herself together sharply!

She knew only too well what the Duke's feelings about her were, and she was quite certain that if he was thinking about her at all, he was considering how he could be rid of her.

If he had taken her to the South of France as he had intended, she was quite certain that after he had left her there he would have found it convenient to forget her very existence.

He was not a Scotsman, and vaguely Jabina thought there must be some way in which he could extricate himself from a marriage into which he had been trapped by force of circumstances.

Perhaps the Scottish law did not apply to Englishmen?

It was all very difficult to contemplate, but at the same time Jabina was certain that whatever happened the Duke would somehow contrive that they need never see each other again.

As he had no wish to marry it would not affect him if he had to remain tied to a woman he never saw.

Yet as far as she was concerned the future was too horrible to contemplate.

To be separated from the man she loved and unable to marry anyone else was a fate, Jabina told herself, that could prove worse than the fires of hell!

She wanted to beg the Duke to think of some alternative, but there was no possibility of their discussing it with the coachman beside them.

Besides there was nothing either of them could do about their predicament until they were safely in England.

Jabina felt a little tremor of fear go through her at the thought that they might never reach the security of their own country.

Even when they arrived at Quillebeuf they had to

find the smugglers, escape the sentries, and cross the Channel, which in itself might prove very difficult.

She remembered hearing stories of the Revenue Cutters firing on smugglers' boats and of smugglers fighting desperately for their lives so that many people were killed in the battle.

Quite suddenly her spirit of adventure left her and she felt weak and afraid. A woman faced by violence!

Then she told herself that somehow the Duke would protect her.

He might be uninterested in her as a woman. Nevertheless he would deem it his duty to keep her from harm.

She remembered how stern he had been the night before, when she wished to go into the Tavern and join in the dancing.

Even now she could not think of the drunken soldiers and their flamboyant women without feeling slightly sick at what she had seen.

She had not realised that people, especially women, ever behaved in such a manner.

She had known soldiers were rough, coarse, and often brutal, but she had never connected the crimes they committed on battle-fields with the sort of licensed indency that she had seen last night through the window on the stairs.

'How could I ever have thought that I could travel across France alone?' she asked herself.

For the first time she realised that the Duke was not being stuffy or repressive when he had averred that she must be chaperoned.

"I must tell him I am sorry I argued about it," she whispered beneath her breath.

As soon as they arrived at the Inn at Quillebeuf Madame Delmas announced that she was going to bed.

"I will have supper upstairs," she said, and the General did not protest.

It was not only that Madame was tired, Jabina found when she helped her undress, but that she intended to look her best when they arrived at Le Havre.

Therefore she required a special beauty mask to be applied to her face and the usual massage to be performed on her feet, hands, and back.

It all took a long time, but at last Jabina was released and she was not only exhausted but hot!

The weather was unexpectedly warm for the month of May.

Leaving Madame Delmas in the darkened room with the blinds lowered, Jabina went up another flight of stairs to the room she had been allotted.

The Inn was not full and she found that her bedchamber was very different from the one she and the Duke had occupied the night before.

It was not in the attic, for one thing. There was other furniture in the room besides the bed and, although the wooden floor was bare, it was polished and clean and there were several small mats.

There was also a wash-stand and Jabina took off her black-serge gown and sponged herself all over.

Then she put on the only other dress she possessed, which was the thin cotton one which she had been told a *femme de chambre* would wear in the morning when she had rough work to do.

Jabina might be reversing the process, but the gown was cool, clean, and very much more becoming than the black dress she had worn all day.

It had a full skirt over a coarse cotton petticoat and the neck was cut low and tied with a draw-string. It had short sleeves and there was a high-fronted apron to wear over it.

A mob-cap in which she could conceal her hair completed the outfit.

Because she felt, now that they had almost reached the end of their journey, it was unlikely that she would be dismissed, Jabina brushed the remaining dark powder from her hair so that it glistened and shone in the fading light coming through the casement.

Far from dismissing her, Madame Delmas had actually expressed some words of approval when Jabina had been massaging her back.

"Your hands are soft," she said, "I cannot imagine that you have done much hard work, Maria."

Jabina had stiffened, wondering if Madame Delmas was suspicious, but the French woman had gone on:

"I want you to keep your hands like that. I hate being touched by rough fingers. My own skin is so sensitive."

"It is indeed, Madame," Jabina murmured.

"I shall therefore inform the household when we reach Le Havre that you are attending exclusively to me," Madame Delmas said. "I will get housemaids to see to the cleaning, the lighting of fires, and the washing. I want you to concentrate only on me and my clothes. Can you sew?"

"Yes, Madame."

"That is good. Even if we are away from Paris, there is no need for me to lose my chic or to degenerate, as so many Army officers' wives do, into proverbial scarecrows."

"I am sure you could never look like that, Madame!" Jabina said, knowing the compliment would please her employer, which it did.

But nothing anyone could do could alter the fact that Madame Delmas's hair was sparse and an unattractive colour.

'No amount of brushing could make it glisten with fiery tongues like mine,' Jabina thought.

Then she remembered that the Duke would be waiting for her, and hastily stuffing her red hair into the mob-cap she went downstairs to find him.

She had not realised it was so late and discovered him in the kitchen trying to hurry an old woman into getting the General's dinner ready.

"Come and help me!" he said to Jabina. "The General is becoming impatient. The Inn-keeper is serving drinks to other travellers and I cannot get this old woman to bestir herself."

"I will help her," Jabina said.

She politely proferred assistance which was gratefully accepted, and soon the old woman, who she discovered was the Inn-keeper's mother, had handed over to her the making of an omelette, while she herself prepared a *Coq-au-vin* and the cold meats which were to follow on the menu.

"Go and lay the table!" Jabina said to the Duke. "Give the General plenty of drink to keep him in a good temper."

"I have been doing that!" the Duke said with a smile.

But he obeyed Jabina and when he came back the omelette was ready.

Jabina turned it out onto a plate and said:

"Hurry! Make him eat it while it is still hot. I will dish up the chicken and you can come back for the cold meats."

Because on his return the Duke was laden with a pigeon-pie, roast of veal, and some large garlic-flavoured sausages, Jabina found herself carrying the dish containing the *Coq-au-vin* into the private parlour where the General was waiting.

It was quite an attractive little room, she noticed, with a huge Breton Cabinet against one wall, an oak dresser on the other, and a long, carved settle with a cushioned seat in front of the open fire-place.

The ceiling was heavily beamed and the flagged floor was liberally covered with rugs.

The whole scene was very picturesque. The General was seated at a small refectory table and there were several empty wine glasses near his elbow.

Turning to Jabina he said:

"Jacques tells me, Maria, that you cooked the omelette."

Jabina nodded.

"It is very good. I can see we shall have to promote you to a place in the kitchen when we reach Le Havre."

"I am afraid Madame will not agree to that, Monsieur," Jabina replied. "She has already told me that she wishes me to attend to her exclusively. But at the same time, Monsieur, I would not wish you to go hungry."

"There appears to be no chance of that tonight at any rate," the General smiled.

The Duke piled dishes on the table around him and Jabina offered him the *Coq-au-vin*.

He helped himself generously, and then Jabina remembered the salad which had been prepared and hurried to the kitchen to collect it.

There were no puddings to follow since the old woman was quite incapable of preparing such delicacies, but there was cheese and fresh fruit. The General expressed himself well satisfied and no longer hungry.

He commanded the Duke to fetch him some cognac from the bar and Jabina piled the dirty dishes onto a tray to carry them away to the kitchen.

"You require coffee, *Monsieur?*" she enquired.

"Yes, I would like coffee," the General replied, "and see you make it yourself."

"Of course, *Monsieur.*"

Jabina went back to the kitchen and met the Duke in the passage carrying a bottle in his hand.

"I have something to tell you," he said in a low voice, "as soon as you have finished."

"The General wants coffee," Jabina said.

"Well hurry and take it to him," the Duke ordered, "and if he wants anything further, then he can fetch it himself!"

"Are you prepared to tell him so?" Jabina teased.

She hurried to the kitchen to brew the coffee, set a cup and saucer on a tray, find a bowl of sugar, and finally to carry it all back down the passage to the private parlour.

The Duke was still with the General, who with a glass of cognac in his hand was standing with his back to the fire-place discoursing on some tactic he had employed in a battle in which he had obviously been extremely successful.

"Ah! My coffee!" he exclaimed as Jabina entered. "That will be all, Jacques. Take my sword and see that it is cleaned by the morning. I thought today the hilt was not as bright as it should be."

"I will do it at once, *Mon Général*," the Duke answered servilely.

He picked up the sword from a side-table where the General had discarded it, attached to his brightly coloured sword-belt.

Putting down the coffee, Jabina would have followed him but the General stopped her by saying:

"Pour my coffee for me. I take two spoon-fuls of sugar."

"Oui, Monsieur."

Jabina did as she was told and carried the coffee cup to the General.

He was looking at her but made no effort to take the coffee cup from her.

"You have a very white skin, Maria," he said after a moment.

"So I have been told, *Monsieur*."

"Are you happy with your husband?"

"Yes, *Monsieur*."

"He is kind to you?"

"Yes indeed, *Monsieur*."

"And he appreciates your white skin?"

There was something in the General's voice which made Jabina feel nervous.

She put the cup down carefully on the small table which stood beside the hearth.

"If there is nothing else you require, *Monsieur*," she said, "I must go and help my husband."

"He can clean a sword without your assistance," the General answered. "Lock the door!"

The order made Jabina jump.

She looked into the General's eyes and knew a sudden fear she had never experienced before.

"Lock the . . . door, *Monsieur*?" she faltered.

"You heard what I said."

"I . . . I think I must . . . go to my . . . husband."

She started to move away but almost as she reached the door, the General said quietly:

"Jacques appears to me to have recovered remarkably well from the wounds inflicted upon him. I think tomorrow it would be wise for me to have him examined by the Medical Officer in Le Havre. If he is well enough, he should be fighting for France."

"Oh no! You cannot do that!" Jabina said, then remembered that by tomorrow she and the Duke might not be there.

As if he almost sensed her thoughts the General added:

"Of course on the other hand, if I thought he was scrimshanking, I could, having warned you of my intention, have him put under arrest tonight. There are soldiers stationed in Quillebeuf. I saw them as we entered the town."

"Why? Why should you want to do this?" Jabina asked almost frantically.

"Lock the door and I will tell you," the General replied.

Trying desperately to think of what to do, and at the same time terrified lest the General should put his threat into action and call the soldiers to take the Duke away, Jabina went slowly to the door.

She thought perhaps she could pull it open and run to the Duke, but she knew to do so would be to put him in danger.

"Lock it and bring me the key," the General said and now there was no doubting the command in his voice.

The lock was a large one and so was the key.

Jabina began obediently to turn it as she had been told, then an idea came to her that she must pretend to do what the General had ordered, yet leave the door unlocked so that she would be able to escape.

She rattled the key in the lock without turning it, pulled it out, and walked across the room with it in her hand.

Her eyes were very wide and frightened in her small face and somehow her brain seemed to have been turned into wool and would not function.

She held out the key to the General and he put out his hand not to take it from her but to pull the mob-cap from her head.

Because she had merely stuffed her hair into the cap and not pinned it up the glittering red tresses fell down over her shoulders.

It seemed to her as if the colour was strangely reflected in the General's eyes.

He looked at her for one moment and then he picked her up in his arms and threw her down on the settle.

For a moment her breath was knocked out of her body at the surprise and roughness of his action.

Then as she gave a scream he threw himself on top of her.

She expected him first to try to kiss her and turned her face away against the hard wooden back of the settle, but instead she felt his hands tear at the neck of her cotton dress, ripping it first from one breast and then the other.

Jabina screamed again.

She felt as if the sound had died in her throat both from her own paralysing fear and the fact that the General was lying on top of her and he was very heavy.

His hands were rough against her bare skin, and as she felt him dragging at her full skirt, she tried to scream again.

Even as she did so, he slumped forward heavily, his forehead hitting hers and knocking her for the moment almost senseless.

A second or so later she felt the General being dragged from off her body and turned her face to see that the Duke was pulling him onto the floor.

Protruding from the very centre of his back, thrust deep into his body, was his own sword.

"Drue! Drue!" Jabina cried.

Now the General's legs were dragged to the floor with a thump.

Jabina tried to sit up, feeling that her muscles would not obey her and aware that she was trembling all over as if with a sudden ague.

Then she was conscious of her naked breasts and felt that she was going to burst into tears.

But before she could do so the Duke's voice rang out sharply—so sharply that it was almost like a dash of cold water in her face:

"Get up and help me! Lock the door in case someone tries to come in."

For a moment Jabina could hardly realise what he was saying until as he dragged the General away from the settle, trembling she rose to her feet and picked up the key of the door where she had dropped it on the floor.

"Lock it and hurry!" the Duke ordered, "and then open that cupboard."

Jabina found it surprising that she could walk.

Somehow she reached the door, turned the key, and looked around to see that the Duke was dragging the dead or unconscious General towards the Breton Cabinet.

She reached it before him and opened the door.

It had obviously been used as a receptacle for coats, because apart from a small shelf at the top, there were only wooden pegs inside it.

The Duke pushed the General in face downwards and then he bent his legs upwards and backwards so that the door could be closed.

He locked it and threw the cupboard key into the fire.

"Let us hope they will not find him there too quickly," he said in what appeared to be a quite normal voice.

Because he seemed so matter-of-fact, Jabina felt her own panic subsiding a little. She still trembled but not so violently.

The Duke took one look at her face and picking up the bottle of cognac that stood on the table, poured some of it into a glass.

"Drink this!"

"No!" Jabina tried to say, but he held the glass to her lips and literally forced it down her throat.

She found herself spluttering as the fiery spirit seared its way into her body.

But she no longer trembled and taking her by the arm the Duke pulled her across the room to the door, unlocked it, looked outside, and then pulled her quickly after him.

He locked the door of the parlour and pushed the key under the door so that it was inside the room.

"That ought to puzzle them!" he said in a low voice. "Come along! We must leave at once."

Jabina was watching wide-eyed, her hands holding up the torn remnants of her cotton bodice.

The Duke looked round.

Hanging in the Hall was the General's overcoat and beside it, because Jabina had not thought to take it upstairs, was the cape edged with sable which Madame Delmas had worn the day before when they'd left Paris.

It had been too hot today for her to need it and had been left in the carriage when she had entered the Inn and proceeded upstairs.

The Duke took the cape down and put it over Jabina's shoulders as he said quietly:

"Take my arm. If anyone sees us they will think we are just going out for a breath of air."

They walked down the passage side by side but, as it happened, encountered no-one.

The old woman was busy in the kitchen and with her was a young girl who she had told Jabina was expected to come in later to wash up.

The Landlord was still serving drinks in the public part of the Inn.

They reached the yard, and now the Duke, looking round quickly, saw an open cart such as farmers used drawn by one horse which was tethered to a post.

He moved quickly towards it—so quickly that Jabina had difficulty in keeping up with him. He lifted her up into the cart, and then untying the horse he led it out from the yard.

There was the sound of laughter and voices.

Through the windows of the Inn Jabina could

perceive a number of men clustered round the bar, but the noise they were making precluded their hearing the wheels of the cart, and she knew that while she could see them, they could not see her.

As soon as they were clear of the Inn and out onto the open road, the Duke climbed into the cart, and picking up the reins whipped the horse into action.

"We have not far to go," he said. "I have already found out that the smugglers come right up the mouth of the river. There is a place about a mile and a half away where they pick up their contraband."

Jabina did not answer and after a moment he said:

"That is what I was going to tell you."

"I . . . I thought you . . . would not hear . . . me scream," Jabina said with a sob.

"It was my fault," the Duke said briefly. "I should not have let you wait on him. These damned Frenchmen are all the same—lecherous swine!"

There was so much violence in his tone that Jabina looked up at him in surprise.

As she did so the Duke pulled the patch from his eye and threw it away.

"Thank God I can be rid of that thing!" he said, "but it did not prevent me seeing the exact place in a man's back where he can be killed with the sharp point of an instrument."

"You . . . killed him with his . . . own sword!" Jabina said in a wondering tone.

"I wish I could have shot him with his own pistol and blown a hole in him with his own cannon!" the Duke said savagely.

"I think I knew all the time that you would . . . save me," Jabina said in a low voice. "At the same time it was . . . horrible! I did not think a man who is supposed to be a gentleman would do that sort of thing."

"You have a lot to learn."

"I know that now," she answered solemnly. "You were right! I . . . I could never have travelled across . . . France alone."

The Duke did not answer and she had the feeling he did not want to talk.

Now that they were through the village he was moving a little more cautiously in the darkness. However it was not too dark for them to be able to see the narrow road which ran along the side of the Seine.

They must have travelled for over a mile when the Duke brought the horse to a stand-still.

"We are going to walk from here," he said. "I have not forgotten what the Duc de St. Croix told us about the sentries."

"Would it not be better to get in touch with the Royalist agents?" Jabina asked. "They know better than we do where the smugglers are likely to be."

"There is no time," the Duke said briefly. "When the General is found the whole countryside will be scoured for us. If we do not get away tonight, Jabina, we can hardly escape being arrested on a charge of murder!"

The Duke spoke very seriously and Jabina shuddered.

"I do not want to frighten you," he said more gently, "but we must not remain in France a minute longer than is necessary."

"No, of course not," she answered.

The Duke helped her down from the cart and turning the horse round set him off in the direction from which they had just come.

Taking Jabina by the hand he started to walk with her along the opposite side of the road from the river.

"Would it not be better to follow the water?" she whispered.

"That is exactly what they would expect a stranger to do," the Duke replied.

They had walked on for some way when suddenly the Duke pulled Jabina down beside a bush.

He put his fingers to her lips as he did so and she realised that she must not speak.

While they had been driving, the stars had come out and there was a pale moon creeping up the sky.

148

It gave very little light but enough for Jabina from where she was crouching to see two soldiers silhouetted against the moonlight, standing with their backs to them, looking down onto the river.

The Duke was very still.

"We have to take a chance," he whispered after a few moments. "Will you go up to the men and tell them that you have lost your dog? Try to persuade one of them to go in search of the animal but keep the one who remains in conversation."

Jabina was still but though he could not see her face the Duke knew she was looking at him.

"Be brave!" he said softly. "If there are any difficulties I swear I will rescue you."

Because she knew he expected it of her, Jabina forced herself to obey him.

She wanted to cling to him, to say she would not leave him, but then she knew he would despise her for being chicken-hearted.

With an effort she straightened herself and stepped into the middle of the road, whistling as she did so.

"Fido! Fido!" she called and whistled again.

She saw the two soldiers turn round sharply at the sound of her voice.

Then one man, who she guessed must be the senior, stepped into the centre of the road and barred her way.

He was about to speak but Jabina forestalled him.

"Oh, *Monsieur* . . . help me! I am in such trouble!"

She pushed back the hood of her cape as she spoke so that he could see her face in the moonlight.

"What is it, *M'mselle?*" he enquired.

"My employer sent me out with her dog for a walk," Jabina said with a most convincing little sob, "and the dog has run away. She will be in such a rage if I cannot find him."

"What is he like?" the soldier asked.

Now the other man who had been watching with him climbed up onto the road to stand beside him.

"He is small and dark and very intelligent," Jabina

answered. "He always comes when I call him. Do you think someone has stolen him?"

"Much more likely he's inside a rabbit-hole," the man said. "Come on, Henri, you have a look round for him. Try whistling."

"I'll do that," the other soldier said. "In which direction did he go, *M'mselle?*"

"I think he went up there," Jabina said, pointing her hand to the side of the road away from the river. "Please whistle very loud. I feel he will not have heard me, not if he was hunting."

"That's more than likely," the Corporal said. "Get going, Henri, you've a way with dogs."

The younger soldier started off, whistling loudly as he went.

Jabina looked up at the Corporal.

"You are very kind," she said. "It is difficult to get employment these days and I do not want to lose my job."

"I'm sure someone will give you another one," the Corporal said in obvious tones of heavy gallantry.

"It is very difficult," Jabina said. "The lady I am with now is very harsh and often unkind to me. But I have my old mother and three sisters to help. My father and brother are both serving in the Army."

"Are they indeed?" the Corporal replied. "And what Regiment are they in?"

Jabina told him the name of the Regiment which was on the Duke's papers.

"Ah! I know it well! A fine crowd—cut to pieces in Austria they were."

"You do not think . . . my father and brother . . . may have been . . . killed?" Jabina asked. "We have not . . . heard from them for a long . . . time."

"No. They will be all right," the Corporal said soothingly, as if he was sorry he had worried her. "It is just that war is war and life is often uncertain."

"It is indeed," Jabina said, "and it must be hard for you having to be out here on duty in the cold night after night."

"We've to look out for spies, and now they tells us there're a whole lot of Tourists trying to escape from France. Blasted English! The sooner they're in prison —the better. That's what I say!"

As the Corporal spoke something hit him hard on the back of the neck. His heard jerked forward as he received another smashing blow from a stone that the Duke applied with such violence that it knocked him completely unconscious.

As the Corporal tumbled to the ground the Duke grabbed Jabina by the hand and ran with her down to the water's edge.

Then still running he dragged her along until just ahead of them she saw a bend in the river and beside it a shed.

It was difficult to see exactly what was there except that there was a light inside the shed. Through an open door she could see men coming in and out carrying bundles on their shoulders.

The Duke, still holding her by the hand, moved nearer and now at last Jabina could see men going down to the river where tied up to the bank she could vaguely discern the outline of a long boat.

Nearer and nearer the Duke crept, keeping first in the shadow of some bushes then some thick rushes which grew down to the water's edge.

" 'Ow much more for this end?" she heard a man say in English with a countryman's broad accent.

"Four more barrels after this lot should fill the stern," another man answered. "Then us'll start on th'bow."

The Duke was motionless and Jabina hardly dared to breathe.

Four men, each carrying a round barrel on his shoulders, piled them into the boat and then went back into the hut.

There was the chatter of voices and as the last man disappeared the Duke pulled Jabina forward.

Keeping well in the shadows of the rushes, he

reached the end of the boat and bending down threw three barrels into the water.

He lifted Jabina into the hole he had made in the cargo, and as she settled herself as comfortably as she could he crept in beside her.

He was only just in his place and hidden by the pile of barrels on each side of them as the men returned.

Jabina trembled with apprehension.

She was well aware that the smugglers would take swift vengeance on anyone who disposed of the cargo for which they had already paid.

Fortunately the man who was giving the orders was occupied in filling the bow with the contraband.

"Keep them bales of baccy in th'middle," he ordered. "We don't want 'em splashed with sea-water."

"Us can't pack in much more!" another man remarked.

"Y'd be surprised wot us can carry!" the man who was giving the orders replied. "Us're all agoing ta make our fortunes out of this little lot an' make no mistake about it!"

"Oi hopes ye be right!" another man said. "But if th' cargo be o'er heavy, us'll not be able ta run from th' Revenue Cutters."

"Stop grousing!" the Head man snarled. " 'Tis unlucky!"

Jabina had the feeling that was a word they did not wish to hear.

They went back to the shed again and now more men came back with more barrels to go into the stern. Jabina could feel the boat sinking lower into the water.

"That be th'lot!" the Head man said. "Tell th'others us be ready. Us don't want ta waste time!"

"Nay," the man who was nervous replied. "Us wants to get 'ome afore it's light."

"Us'll be back long afor' that!" the Head man replied.

Jabina made herself a little more comfortable.

There was only very little room for her to sit, and she was so close to the Duke that only by putting his arms round her could they both squeeze into the space he had made by removing the barrels.

The men came running from the shed.

It was difficult to count them, but Jabina thought there must be twenty oarsmen. That meant that the boat was a large one and they should cross the Channel more swiftly than if it had been one of the smaller type.

A Frenchman must have come to see them off because as they started to move, pushing the boat away from the bank with their oars, a voice speaking in broken English said:

"Au 'voir, messieurs! Bon chance! We'll be looking out for you next week."

"Us'll be with ye, Frenchy!" one of the oarsmen cried and then they were moving down the river.

"How did ye do?" Jabina heard one of the men ask.

"Well enough," was the reply. "They drives an 'ard bargain, these Froggies, but they wants ta trade agin now that th'war 'as started oop. They needs our gold, as us well knows. They be prepared ta sell anything for it. Even Jos'phine, if us asked for 'er!"

There was laughter at this.

Then the Head man said sharply:

"Ye can laugh when ye are 'ome an' safe. Get on with it now. There's be a wind agetting oop, and if it be choppy Oi don't want any of ye athrowing oop."

"Us be too nervous t'be sick, Bill," one of the men replied.

They settled down to rowing and there was no doubt that they were proficient, for they swept down the river quickly and quite soon Jabina could feel waves slapping against the sides of the boat.

Once they were out in mid-Channel it began to be choppy and she was thankful that she did not suffer from sea-sickness.

Now the oarsmen were silent except for occasional grunts and groans as they sweated at the oars, using every ounce of muscle into getting their cargo back safely.

At the same time they were heavy-laden and they must have been able to move much more swiftly on the outward journey.

Jabina began to feel desperately cramped but she dared not move.

She thought that perhaps the Duke was even more uncomfortable than she was, because she could lean against him and his encircling arm cushioned her from the barrels which moved occasionally from the roughness of the sea.

Jabina put her head against the Duke's shoulder and shut her eyes. She tried to pretend to herself that he was holding her close because he wished to do so.

She thought that if he bent his head only a little it would be easy for him to kiss her. She could feel his lips against hers!

She felt herself quiver at the thought, and because the Duke must have thought she was cold he tightened his arm and with his free hand pulled her cloak closer around her.

She loved him because he was being kind and considerate to her.

She could not have imagined it possible that a man could kill to save her honour.

The mere thought of the General's hands on her breasts made her feel again the horror and terror that he had evoked in her.

The weight of his body on hers had made her feel paralysed with fear, and she knew now that but for the Duke's intervention she would have been ravished. Although what that actually entailed she was not quite certain!

She only knew that it would have frightened her almost to death!

Thinking of the soldiers she had seen in the Tavern last night and of the General's behaviour tonight, she felt very young and very ignorant.

'How could I ever have done anything so foolish as to run away from home?' she asked herself now, 'and imagined I could look after myself in the outside world?'

For the first time since she had met the Duke it occurred to her to wonder what would have happened to her had he been like the General.

Perhaps she might even have encountered the same sort of soldiers who were behaving so indecently in the Tavern.

How incredibly fortunate she had been that it was the Duke who had given her a seat in his carriage and then carried her in his yacht to France.

He had protected her and kept her safe from many evils of which she had been totally unaware before.

She knew that all her life she would be haunted by the memory of the sword sticking out of the General's back and of the Duke dragging him across the floor to the Breton Cabinet.

He had killed a man to save her!

It was as if the shock of what she had been through had at last begun to make itself felt and the effect of the brandy was no longer sustaining.

Quite suddenly Jabina wanted to cry.

She wanted to sob her heart out because she had been frightened, because the Duke had saved her, and because she wanted him to understand how grateful she was.

Then she knew she must somehow control herself. She might make a noise if she cried and the smugglers would discover them.

Jabina had the idea that should they be discovered the smugglers would have no compunction in throwing them both overboard, just as the Duke had thrown the barrels into the water to make a place for them.

If that should happen no-one would ever know what had become of them.

They would be dead and perhaps soon forgotten.

'I must not let my imagination run away with me,' Jabina told herself as she had done so often before.

But this time she knew the danger they were in was

very real, and until they actually reached the shores of England, they must be on their guard.

'Please, God, let us get there!' Jabina found herself praying.

And then with her cheek against the Duke's shoulder she whispered in her heart:

'And please let Drue . . . like me a . . . little . . . let him not wish to get . . . rid of me too . . . quickly . . . please God.'

Chapter Eight

The hours passed slowly and Jabina found herself growing sleepy.

The motion of the boat rocked by the waves and the strong sea-air made it hard for her to keep her eyes open. Moreover, there was nothing in front of her but the sight of wooden barrels.

Her legs felt cramped and began to ache. She was quite certain that the Duke was experiencing the same discomfort as his arms were round her.

But it was impossible for either of them to move and after a time she deliberately tried not to think or to be afraid, but rather to hypnotise herself into a kind of oblivion of everything but the closeness of the Duke's body to her own.

She tried to remember how long it took to cross the Channel and she had a feeling somewhere in the back of her mind that in faster boats smugglers could go from Dover to Calais in three hours.

She was certain however that the boat in which they were travelling was so heavily laden that it would take longer.

Then she started to dream and she was back in the parlour of the Inn and the General had thrown himself on top of her.

She could feel the weight of him on her body and she opened her lips to scream.

The Duke, with an extraordinary perception, must

157

have known what was happening, for he covered her mouth with his hand and Jabina awoke with a start.

She felt his fingers warm against her cold lips and knew that he had saved her from revealing their hiding-place.

I am . . . sorry, she wanted to say, but knew she must not speak and instead looked up at him pleadingly as he took his hand from her mouth realising she was at last fully awake.

She was aware now that she could see his face, although only indistinctly through the luminous softness of a morning mist.

The night was over. It must be nearly dawn and above them the stars would be disappearing. Soon the first fingers of the sun would sweep away the last darkness of the night.

'Thank Heaven for the mist,' Jabina thought, aware that it would hide them from being seen as they neared the Coast of England.

She had a feeling that the Duke was smiling at her, but she could not be sure.

She only felt his arm tighten as if in re-assurance, and then his fingers that had covered her mouth touched her face gently as if to tell her that all was well.

His face was very near to hers and she had a sudden longing to put her cheek against his or even to kiss it.

'Would he understand that I am showing my gratitude?' she wondered.

Then she feared that if she did such a thing, he would stiffen as she had seen him do before.

Then there would be the same expression of disdain and contempt on his face as there had been when he had raged at her in the Inn in Scotland and told her that he had no wish to be married.

She could remember so well the words he had used then, and the thought came back to her accusingly as if he said them all over again:

"An irritating, impulsive, half-witted chit is not the type of wife I require."

Jabina had hoped he would change his mind about her, but she was now quite certain that he had not done so.

If he had grown to care for her in the slightest, would he not have shown some sign of it when they had shared the bed-room together at Verdon?

Would he not have held her in his arms and kissed her after the General had frightened her and they had hidden his body in the Breton Cabinet?

Instead the Duke had simply marched her out of the Inn and hurried her away in the farm cart to where they had finally been able to hide themselves in the smugglers' boat.

'Even now,' she thought, 'when we are so near home and his arms are round me, he has not made any gesture of affection.'

It would be so easy for him just to kiss her forehead and tell her without words that he knew she was frightened but that he would protect her.

'I am nothing to him! Nothing!' Jabina told herself despairingly.

She looked up at him again, her eyes searching through the mist to see him clearly, and she thought in fact it was now easier to see him than it had been a moment ago.

In that very second there was the sound of a boat approaching them and a voice called out:

"Heave to—in the name of His Majesty King George III—and identify yourselves."

The words came sharply through the mist and, even as they died away, from the other side of their boat there was a splash of oars and a second voice shouted hoarsely:

"Identify yourselves in the name of His Majesty. This is a Revenue Cutter and if we do not receive an answer from you we will open fire."

"Oh me God!" one of the oarsmen gasped. "Us be trapped! 'Tis th'gallows for we!"

"Aye, us be trapped!" another man groaned.

Then, to Jabina's astonishment, the Duke struggled to his feet and, holding on to the barrels in front of him in order to keep his balance, he said:

"Leave this to me," and shouting into the mist called out: "I am the Duke of Warminster escaping from France. We need your assistance in finding a place to land."

There was silence before an audible gasp which Jabina knew was one of astonishment.

Then she heard the Duke say in a low voice to the men in front of him:

"Drop the cargo overboard—and quickly!"

She was sure they must have been as astonished by the Duke's announcement as the Revenue Cutters were.

Then through the mist a voice called:

"Give your name again! Did you say you had escaped from France?"

"Yes! I enlisted the help of these men to bring me to England," the Duke replied. "As I said before, I am the Duke of Warminster and need your protection. Kindly show us where to land."

The smugglers were busy throwing the bales of tobacco and the barrels of brandy into the sea.

Each one went in with a splash. Then as several men cleared the stern while others started on what was in the bow, they saw Jabina and stared at her with their mouths open.

"Hurry!" the Duke said in an urgent voice. "The mist is clearing. They will be able to see us shortly."

The men re-doubled their efforts, the boat rocking precariously as they jettisoned the barrels one after the other.

"You will find Seaford Creek to your North-West," a voice boomed from the Revenue Cutter. "Do not go further North or you will be on the cliffs! We are close beside you so do not try to evade us."

They were not certain, Jabina thought, that the Duke's reply had not been a trick of the smugglers to evade capture.

At the same time she felt that those in charge of the Revenue Cutters must have been impressed by the cultured tones of his voice and the authority with which he spoke.

"We are obeying your instructions," the Duke answered.

He seated himself in the bow as, with the boat now empty of its cargo, the men picked up their oars.

The barrels of brandy had sunk easily, but the bales of tobacco had not yet disappeared.

Jabina could see the smugglers looking at them anxiously.

The fat bales were floating on the tide and some of them were drifting in towards the shore.

"Let us get away from here as quickly as possible," the Duke said in a low voice.

The men started to pull at the oars, turning as they had been directed towards the North-West.

Now it was light enough to see their faces, and Jabina, pulling her cloak closely round her, realised they looked a coarse and indeed villainous crew.

She was quite convinced that had she and the Duke been discovered before the arrival of the Revenue Cutters, they would have been dealt with roughly if not violently and might in fact have lost their lives.

" 'Ow did ye get in th'boat without us anoticing ye?" a man asked the Duke.

"The less we say the better!" the Duke replied. "Voices carry on the water. Leave the talking to me and you shall not go unrewarded in effecting my rescue and that of the lady with me."

"If ye give us away," one of the men said, "they'll hang us—or it'll be transportation!"

"Just leave it to me," the Duke answered.

When the man would have spoken again the Head man hushed him into silence.

The mist cleared suddenly and Jabina saw ahead of them a wide creek with marsh-land beyond the cliffs sloping down to it on either side.

The smugglers turned into the still water and hardly were they away from the sea when the two Revenue Cutters appeared behind them.

They ran a little way up the creek and the front oarsmen jumped ashore to steady the boat while the others, having shipped their oars, straightened their backs and stepped out onto the muddy bank.

The Duke followed suit and lifting Jabina in his arms carried her clear of the mud and on to some grass.

Having set her down he walked down the creek to where the Commander of the first Revenue Cutter had come ashore.

"I am exceedingly grateful for your assistance, Officer," he said, "and still more grateful to have escaped from France."

"You are indeed the Duke of Warminster?" the Officer enquired.

"I am!" the Duke said with a smile. "As I expect you know, Bonaparte has ordered the arrest and imprisonment of every Tourist who was in France on the eighteenth of May."

"We heard that was what he had done," the Officer replied. "We could hardly believe it!"

"I can assure you that it is true!" the Duke answered. "This lady and I managed to escape from Paris in disguise. When we reached the Coast these men were kind enough to convey us home."

There was a faint smile on the Revenue Officer's lips as he looked at the smugglers standing awkwardly by their boat.

There would be no mistaking, Jabina thought, their motive for having crossed the Channel and they certainly looked the kind of desperate gang who would take any risk to bring back the contraband from which they could make so much profit.

The Officer looked them over and then turned to the Duke.

"As their boat is empty, Your Grace," he said, "I have no evidence of course that they were moving along the Coast of France except on an errand of mercy."

The Duke smiled in return.

"I am extremely obliged to them."

"I am sure of that, Your Grace!" the Officer replied. "I cannot believe the French prisons are particularly comfortable!"

The Duke put out his hand.

"Thank you," he said, "and perhaps you would be gracious enough to thank on my behalf whoever is in charge of your other Cutter. I assure you both that I shall notify the Lords of the Admiralty of the service you have done me."

"I thank Your Grace," the Officer said.

The Duke walked a few paces to the leader of the smugglers' crew.

"I can show you my gratitude in a more practical form," he said. "I have with me enough money to reward each of your men with five pounds for the part they played in my rescue. I will also give you a 'note of hand' for a further hundred pounds which can be collected from any Bank in the vicinity."

The expressions on the men's faces were almost ludicrous.

"That's real sportin' of Yer Grace," the Head man said. "Us won't pretend that th'dumping o' th'cargo be not a grievous loss."

"Another time you might be caught red-handed," the Duke warned. "Surely the penalties are too high for it to be worth your while."

"There's always a sportin' chance, Yer Grace, and th'rewards when us can keep away from th'Revenue Cutters be high too."

The Duke did not continue to argue. Instead he drew the money from his inside pocket and wrote out a 'note of hand,' putting his signature to it.

"Should you have any difficulty cashing this," he said, "please let me know. Tonight at any rate I shall be staying at Seaford Park. Do you know it?"

"Aye, Yer Grace. 'Tis but three mile from 'ere."

"I thought that was about the distance," the Duke said. "What I do not know is how I can convey the lady there, and indeed myself. The amount of leg-room we had in your boat last night has left us both somewhat cramped!"

"Oi can fetch two of th'ponies for Yer Grace," the Head man suggested. "They'll not be far away. This be where us were t'land."

"Two ponies would suit us admirably!" the Duke replied.

The Head man turned away to give instructions to the oarsmen.

By now the Revenue Cutters had moved out of the creek back to the sea and it was obvious that in a few seconds they would be out of sight.

The Head man set off across the marsh-land.

The oarsmen lifted the boat out of the water and carried it up the creek for a short distance.

Then to Jabina's surprise they disappeared!

She realised that in the shrubs and rough land lead-ing down to the creek there was a hiding-place which was doubtless one they used habitually.

They were out of view for a short time and then they reappeared one by one but not to return to where she was waiting. Instead they walked away quickly.

Because it was still not completely daylight they were soon out of sight.

The Duke turned towards Jabina.

"We are home!" he said softly.

"I was so afraid we would be discovered," she an-swered.

"Fortune was on our side," he replied, "and now we have only a short way to go to return to the com-forts of civilisation!"

Jabina could not answer, feeling a sudden pang of unhappiness because he seemed so pleased at returning to the world he knew.

"If you are wondering," the Duke went on as she did not speak, "who lives at Seaford Park, there again luck is with us, for it belongs to my cousin, Sir Geof-frey Minster. He is the Member of Parliament for this part of the world."

"That will be nice for you," Jabina said in a low voice.

"I very much doubt if Sir Geoffrey is here at the moment," the Duke said. "With the Declaration of War, Parliament will be sitting and he will be in London and I expect his wife will be with him. But they would, I know, be only too glad for us to avail ourselves of their hospitality in their absence."

As the Duke spoke there appeared through the mist with almost startling suddenness two ponies led by a boy and with the Head man walking beside them.

"Here they be, Yer Grace," he said to the Duke. "Th'boy 'ill show ye th'way."

"I am most grateful to you," the Duke answered.

He pressed some gold coins into the man's hand and then he lifted Jabina onto the first pony and mounted the other himself.

They were small but sure-footed, the kind of sturdy animal most useful in carrying heavy loads of contraband to some secret place of hiding from which it could be conveyed to London.

The boy made no attempt to lead them but they followed him and he walked with confidence across the marshy land until they reached the firm grassy turf of the Downs.

The mist was patchy: one moment they could see glimpses of landscape, the next it was soft and wet against their cheeks.

Then as they appeared to be rising to higher ground there was sun-shine and the whole beauty of the Sussex landscape lay in front of them.

Jabina let her hood fall back from her head because the fur around her face made her feel hot.

She had the feeling that Madame Delmas would be exceedingly annoyed at losing her expensive and valuable cloak, but perhaps it would pale into unimportance beside the fact that she had also lost her husband.

Jabina tried to feel sorry for her, but the memory

of the General made her shudder at the manner in which he had treated her.

'He deserved to die!' she told herself.

It was impossible to talk intimately to the Duke with the boy in charge of the ponies within ear-shot and so they rode in silence.

Travelling first over the Downs and then along twisting narrow roads with cultivated fields on either side they came in sight of the roofs of houses and the high steeple of a Church.

But before they reached the village they came to an important wrought-iron gateway with a Lodge on either side.

The boy led the way through them and they found themselves going up a long drive of ancient oak trees.

This brought them in sight of Seaford Park, a beautiful Elizabethan building with gabled roofs and small diamond-paned windows glinting in the sunshine.

"How pretty!" Jabina exclaimed.

"And it is as comfortable as it looks!" the Duke promised her. "I know that what you want more than anything else at the moment is a chance to sleep."

"It is still very early in the morning," Jabina said. "I wonder if anyone will be awake?"

She need not have worried.

There was a mob-capped maid scrubbing the stone steps who stared at them in surprise as they drew up outside the front door.

She fetched a footman in his shirt-sleeves, who hurried away to return with an elderly man correctly attired, to whom the Duke said:

"Good-morning, Bateman! I dare say you are surprised to see me, but I have in fact just arried from France, this lady and I having escaped imprisonment by the French."

"Your Grace is very welcome," Bateman said respectfully. "I regret that Sir Geoffrey and Her Ladyship departed to London four days ago."

"I thought that would be the case," the Duke answered, "but I am sure in their absence you will look after us, Bateman?"

"I will indeed, Your Grace."

"What we require at the moment is sleep," the Duke said. "A smugglers' boat is not particularly comfortable."

"A smugglers' boat, Your Grace?"

"It was the only transport we could find, Bateman," the Duke said with a smile, "and indeed we were very glad to see it."

"I can well imagine that, My Lord!"

Bateman bowed to Jabina.

"If you could come this way, Ma'am, the House-keeper, Mrs. Dangerfield will attend to you."

Jabina felt a sudden reluctance to leave the Duke, but there was nothing she could do but follow the Butler upstairs.

There he handed her over to a rather awe-inspiring House-keeper who came bustling down the corridor still fastening her gown and obviously agitated at being fetched from her bed-room so early in the morning.

She ushered Jabina into a large bed-room with a huge four-poster bed in keeping with the period of the house, trimmed with flounced muslin which was echoed by a dressing-table similarly adorned.

"How attractive this is!" Jabina exclaimed.

Then because she suddenly felt completely exhausted, she allowed the House-keeper to help her undress.

She slipped into a borrowed night-gown which was far prettier than anything she had ever owned herself, and climbed into the comfortable bed and shut her eyes.

She heard the House-keeper moving around the room drawing the curtains and tut-tutting disapprovingly over the torn condition of her gown. But she was too tired to think up a plausible explanation or even worry what the woman thought.

Almost before the door closed and she was alone she fell asleep.

Jabina awoke because people were moving about the room. For a moment she thought it was inconsiderate of them to disturb her.

But opening her eyes she saw two house-maids carrying in pans of water for a bath that had been arranged on the hearth-rug in front of a small fire.

She lay looking at them, and then the House-keeper came to the side of the bed.

"His Grace has suggested, Ma'am, that you might wish to dine with him."

"Dine?" Jabina exclaimed. "Is it as late as that?"

The House-keeper smiled.

"You've slept for nearly nine hours, Ma'am!"

"I was so tired," Jabina said. "But I would like to dine with His Grace."

"Feeling that was what you'd wish, Ma'am," the House-keeper replied, "there's a bath prepared for you and we can then choose a gown from Her Ladyship's wardrobe in which you can go downstairs."

"I certainly cannot wear the clothes in which I crossed the Channel," Jabina said with a smile. "His Grace and I had to escape in disguise, as I expect you have gathered. I was a *femme de chambre* . . . a lady's-maid!"

"I can't believe it!" Mrs. Dangerfield said holding up her hands in horror. "And His Grace?"

"A valet. And very proficient he was!"

"I can't imagine how you endured such hardships, Ma'am," Mrs. Dangerfield said, "but then one can expect anything of them foreigners."

She spoke with such disgust in her voice that Jabina could not help laughing.

She made no other explanations of their plight but stepped into the warm bath scented with rose-water and felt that she washed away not only the dirt and discomfort of the journey, but also her fear.

It was only now that she realised how frightened she had been, not only at the thought of being captured and put in prison, but also directly by the people she had encountered on their journey.

There had been the drunken soldiers, the General, and the smugglers with their desperate, villainous faces all to make her tremble.

Yet Jabina knew that, though now she was safely back in England, one fear remained.

The fear for her future and what lay ahead of her once she must leave the Duke.

'Perhaps England,' Jabina thought despairingly, 'will prove as frightening as France.'

She remembered what had happened when she ran away from the Duke at the Scottish Inn and the drunken man in the kilt had stolen her money.

She still had her mother's jewellery to prevent her from setting off penniless on her own.

And yet if there were thieves and robbers waiting to snatch it from her, how long would that last?

She felt as she bathed and dressed as if a thousand questions pressed themselves on her mind for which she could find no answer.

She only knew she was afraid and that the future seemed very dark and ominous.

Mrs. Dangerfield produced an elegant, gossamer-thin silk chemise exquisitely embroidered and trimmed with lace.

Then she opened the doors of a big wardrobe which stood at one end of the room and revealed a multitudinous collection of gowns all in beautiful colours which seemed as alluring as a rainbow.

"I'm afraid Her Ladyship is slightly larger than you in the waist, Ma'am," Mrs. Dangerfield said, "but I can easily stitch you into the gown for the evening, and once I've your measurements I can alter something for you to wear on the morrow."

"I do hope Her Ladyship will not mind," Jabina said anxiously.

"Her Ladyship'll be only too glad to be of help, Ma'am, and I know that both she and Sir Geoffrey will be longing to hear of yours and His Grace's adventures."

Mrs. Dangerfield gave a little snort and added:

"It's the only good thing I've ever heard of them

smugglers. A real menace they are in the neighbour-
hood, giving us all a bad name."

Jabina wanted to laugh at the indignation on Mrs.
Dangerfield's face.

Then she realised that to live side by side with the
smugglers with their nefarious goings-on might indeed
be very unpleasant.

"We could not have got home without them," she
said gently.

"Then we must be grateful to them, Ma'am," Mrs.
Dangerfield answered. "Now what colour gown would
you wish to wear for dinner?"

It was very hard to choose from so many and
they were all so lovely.

Jabina was interested to see that while the new fashion she had discovered in Paris had not reached Scotland, Lady Minster's gowns were all high-waisted and
very nearly, if not quite, as transparent as those that
were the vogue amongst French ladies.

Finally she chose a white dress which reminded her
of the beautiful evening-gown she had had to leave
behind in Paris.

It was heart-breaking to think she would never wear
the silver-threaded gauze again with its silver ribbons
in which she had danced with the Duke.

Lady Minster's gown was however nearly as attractive.

It was embroidered with tiny bunches of pearls, and
the ribbons which crossed over the bodice and held the
waist so high were also covered in pearls.

There were three rows of deep lace at the hem and
what was almost an apology for sleeves was also made
of lace.

"It's very becoming to you, Ma'am," Mrs. Dangerfield said with a note of sincerity in her voice.

She made the waist at least two inches tighter and
then she arranged Jabina's hair almost as skilfully as
the French *coiffeusse* had done.

"How clever of you to know the very latest vogue
from Paris!" Jabina exclaimed.

"We're not behind the times in England," Mrs. Dangerfield replied reprovingly, "in fact I've always believed, Ma'am, that it's the English Ladies of Quality who create the fashions and not the wife of that monster and murderer!"

Jabina knew that Bonaparte had been depicted for years as an ogre who would not be above turning cannibal if it suited him!

She repressed a desire to say that she had found France very sophisticated and civilised, knowing that Mrs. Dangerfield would not understand.

'People believe what they want to believe,' Jabina told herself and almost instantly her thoughts went back to the Duke.

He wanted to believe in austerity! He wanted the quiet, uneventful life he had chosen for himself.

She was quite certain that what they had experienced these last days would not change him.

The Vicomte had said it was her opportunity to help him, but she had failed.

She had known it, she thought, when he had introduced her on their arrival not as his wife as he might have done, but just as someone with whom he was travelling.

She had been the Duchess of Warminster in Scotland, his sister, Lady Jabina Minster on the yacht, and in France, his wife again—Maria Boucher. But now she was only 'a Lady,' anonymous, nobody of any importance.

She felt with despair that Fate had treated her harshly.

She had really had no opportunity to make him love her. She had not had the chance of changing him as the Vicomte had suggested she should do, and which she might have succeeded in accomplishing had they stayed on in Paris.

She thought of all the things she had wanted to do, to see, to learn.

The Duke had enjoyed that day at Chantilly when

he had shown her the Prince's garden and the treasures kept in the Benedictine Abbey.

She was sure that he would have liked explaining to her the pictures in the Louvre, the treasures in the Tivoli, and the esoteric beauty of Notre Dame.

But she knew that what she wanted above all things was to dance with him again.

She remembered how well he had danced and how there had seemed to be a new light in his eyes as they waltzed under the lanterns to the noisy Band in the Dance-Garden.

He had seemed much younger at that moment and then she had been stupid enough to spoil the evening by lying to him about the Frenchmen who, she said, had tried to kiss her.

She had known the Duke hated her to exaggerate, yet she had done so simply because she was piqued by his indifference to her appearance. And in doing so she had swept away the mood in which he seemed so different and had incensed him.

"I must be very careful tonight," Jabina told herself.

When finally she was ready she took a last look in the mirror and thought how very different she appeared from the untidy, badly-dressed girl who had thrust herself upon the Duke in Scotland.

Would he appreciate the fact that she was more sophisticated, more poised, and, she hoped, more attractive?

She waited for the answer in her imagination but it was not very encouraging.

Very slowly she descended the oak-carved staircase, crossed the Hall with its Elizabethan-panelled walls and open Mediaeval fire-place.

A flunky opened the door and she passed through it into a beautiful Salon with long windows opening onto a garden.

The walls were hung with pictures, and chandeliers glittering with tapers illuminated the gilt-framed furniture upholstered in pale turquoise blue.

But Jabina had eyes only for the Duke, who was

standing at the far end of the room against the mantel-shelf.

He turned as she entered and once again she saw him as he had appeared in Paris.

His clothes might be borrowed from his cousin but they certainly made him appear as elegant and fashionable as he had looked for one brief evening after he had cast aside his austere black.

His cravat was dazzlingly white against his face tanned from the sun and the sea winds, the points of his collar were high above his chin.

The blue satin evening-coat he was wearing seemed to accentuate the colour of his eyes and the pale champagne-coloured pantaloons fitted him to perfection.

"Oh, I did hope to see you looking like that again!" Jabina exclaimed irrepressibly.

The Duke smiled and taking her hand raised it to his lips.

"May I also congratulate you on your change of wardrobe?" he answered.

"Your cousin and his wife have been very generous in their absence," Jabina said.

"As they would have been had they been here," the Duke answered. "You are rested?"

"I slept for nearly nine hours!" Jabina confessed.

"I too slept well," the Duke said, "and now I am so hungry I could eat anything and anywhere! But I am grateful that we have neither to cook nor serve it!"

Jabina laughed but before she could reply Bateman announced that dinner was ready.

The meal was delicious and the Duke sampled every dish that was offered to him.

Jabina however found that after having eaten a certain amount the anxiety that she was feeling and the fact that there was an exquisite pleasure in being alone with the Duke took away her appetite.

It was difficult to talk intimately with the servants and the Butler in the room.

So the Duke discussed with her the menace of the

173

smugglers who carried gold to Napoleon and told her tales of the gangs which were so ferocious that the villagers and even the Revenue Officers themselves were afraid of them.

He also outlined the measures the Government would have to take to suppress the trade which damaged the country's economy.

Jabina listened intently.

At the same time she knew that always at the back of her mind there were only personal problems.

While she longed to listen to the Duke and give him her whole-hearted concentration, she could not help wondering all the time whether this was the last dinner they would eat alone together and what he would decide to do the following day.

The dessert was cleared from the table and Bateman poured out a glass of port for the Duke.

"You do not wish me to leave you?" Jabina asked anxiously. "I know it is correct."

"I have a better solution to the problem," the Duke said with a smile. "I will bring my port into the Salon where we can sit and talk."

"I'll carry it there for Your Grace," Bateman said solicitously.

He placed the decanter and glass on a salver and followed them down the passage to the Salon.

The curtains had been drawn while they were at dinner, with the exception of one window which opened onto the terrace outside.

There was the fragrance of roses from the garden and Jabina could see the stars were coming out in the darkness of the sky.

She remembered how last night they had lighted their way along the river to where they had found the smugglers' boat.

Bateman handed the Duke his glass of port, set the decanter on a side-table, and then left the Salon, closing the door behind him.

The Duke, standing with his back to the fire-place,

looked at Jabina, but she found it impossible to meet his eyes.

"I think now we should talk about ourselves," he said in a quiet voice.

"Yes ... we ... must!"

Then as if she could not bear what he had to say she walked to the open window to stare out into the darkening garden.

She had the feeling that this was the end! This was the moment she had been dreading not only today and yesterday but every moment since she had left Scotland.

In fact ever since the Duke had saved her from the drunken Scot and taken her under his protection.

She felt as if a stone lay heavy in her breast as she waited, knowing that what he had to say to her now would seem like a death-knell; a sentence which would destroy her happiness and against which she would have no appeal.

She had an almost insane impulse to run away; not to hear him speak but to go out into the darkness of the garden and vanish.

Then she knew she had to listen and that this was the end of everything she had hoped for and longed for, of everything which she had prayed in her heart might change him so that he would care for her a little.

"I am waiting to talk to you, Jabina," the Duke said. "It is difficult to have a conversation with the back of someone's head!"

As if his words stung her into action Jabina turned round.

For one moment she looked at him standing so elegantly, so fashionable and so handsome on the hearth-rug. Then without thinking she ran towards him impetuously.

"Please ... please ..." she cried, "do not ... send me ... away! Let me ... stay with you. I will not be a ... nuisance. No-one will know ... who I am ... I can ... be a ... house-maid or something ... only let me stay."

She saw an expression in the Duke's eyes which she did not understand.

Then, as she felt he was about to refuse her request, she turned quickly away so that he would not see the tears that flooded her eyes and went back towards the window.

She stood fighting against the tempest that threatened to break her control and leave her sobbing hysterically at his feet.

Then she heard his voice just behind her and she had not realised that he had moved.

"My ridiculous, impetuous, adorable little wife," he said in a voice she had never heard before. "Do you really think you would make a good house-maid?"

He turned her round to face him.

But as she tried to see him through the tears which stung her eyes, he swept her crushingly into his arms, holding her so tightly she could not breathe and his lips were on hers.

For a moment Jabina was too surprised to feel anything.

Then something wild and exciting leapt within her and seemed to consume her so that she felt her whole body melt into his.

Her lips clung to his and she knew an ecstasy and rapture such as she did not imagine one could experience and not die of the wonder of it.

He raised his mouth from hers and because she was so bemused she stammered incoherently:

"I—I did not . . . know y-you could kiss like . . . t-that."

"But I can!" the Duke answered, and he was kissing her again, demandingly, possessively, passionately.

The world seemed to circle round Jabina and the ground was no longer solid beneath her feet.

'The Vicomte was right,' she thought. 'The fire was only dampened down and now it has burst into flame.'

Then the Duke's kisses were a wonder which swept away all thought of self and she was a part of him and he of her and they were one.

Downstairs the grandfather clock in the Hall struck two. In the big comfortable bed a soft voice asked:

"When did you first know you loved me?"

The Duke drew her a little closer.

"I fell in love," he answered, "with a very small, cold foot and a tear which splashed on my hand as I was warming it."

"My foot!" Jabina exclaimed. "I had hoped you would say it was my beautiful face!"

The Duke gave a little laugh.

"Your face is fascinating, entrancing and altogether irresistible, my darling, but not really beautiful."

"O-o-oh!" Jabina exclaimed. "Say that again! I never thought that you could say such marvellous things to me!"

"I love you," the Duke said. "Oh my precious, my darling little love, I adore you."

Jabina thrilled to the deep note in his voice; it was like waves of quicksilver rippling through her body.

"I love you . . . too," she whispered.

"Am I too old?"

"No. You are *exactly* the right age!"

"Am I dull and boring?"

"You are the most exciting, adventurous man in the whole word."

She gave a deep sigh of happiness.

"When I think that you . . . killed a man for me I can hardly believe it!"

"I only hope I do not have to kill a number of others," the Duke replied. "I shall be an exceedingly jealous husband, my naughty one!"

"But I am going to be a very good and perfect wife, exactly as you want me to be," Jabina protested.

The Duke laughed.

"I very much doubt it! At the same time I shall make you behave because we have so many things to do together."

"What sort of things?"

"There is work for me to do in the House of Lords," the Duke answered, "and I believe too I can be of service to the War Office. And we must keep our promise."

"What promise?" Jabina enquired.

"To help the Royalists. I think we owe them that."

"But of course," Jabina said. "Can we really help them?"

"We can try," the Duke replied, "and we will both of us work in every way we can to rid the world of Bonaparte."

"It is all so exciting, so perfect," Jabina murmured. "I was so desperately afraid you would send me away."

"I was afraid you might wish to leave me," the Duke said.

"How could you imagine that? I wanted to be with you every second after I knew I was in love with you. I love you so madly it has been agony to think you did not care for me."

"We will never be unsure of each other again," the Duke said firmly.

He felt her body quiver against him and turned towards her.

"Tell me again you love me," he commanded masterfully.

"I love you . . . wildly . . . completely . . . with all of . . . me."

He kissed her forehead, her eyes, and the tip of her little nose.

"Have you . . . ever . . . loved anyone . . . more than me?" she asked.

"I know now I have never loved anyone before! You have crept into my heart, my darling, and I can never be free of you."

His hand was touching her and the breath came quickly between her parted lips.

"You . . . excite me . . ." she whispered.

"I want to excite you."

"It is . . . wonderful! And I know now how . . . marvellous it is when two people are in . . . bed together and they . . . love each other."

"I told you it was nice," the Duke said.

"Nice!" Jabina exclaimed scornfully. "It is glorious! Miraculous! Divine! It is like flying to the moon and holding all the stars in one's arms."

She paused to ask a little humbly:

"Am I . . . exaggerating?"

"No, my precious, that describes it exactly," the Duke answered.

Then his lips possessed her and there was only a fire rising within them both and the wonder of the stars.

ABOUT THE AUTHOR

BARBARA CARTLAND, the celebrated romantic author, historian, playwright, lecturer, political speaker and television personality, has now written over 150 books. Miss Cartland has had a number of historical books published and several biographical ones, including that of her brother, Major Ronald Cartland, who was the first Member of Parliament to be killed in the War. This book had a Foreword by Sir Winston Churchill.

In private life, Barbara Cartland, who is a Dame of the Order of St. John of Jerusalem, has fought for better conditions and salaries for Midwives and Nurses. As President of the Royal College of Midwives (Hertfordshire Branch), she has been invested with the first Badge of Office ever given in Great Britain, which was subscribed to by the Midwives themselves. She has also championed the cause for old people and founded the first Romany Gypsy Camp in the world.

Barbara Cartland is deeply interested in Vitamin Therapy and is President of the British National Association for Health.

Bantam Book Catalog

It lists over a thousand money-saving bestsellers originally priced from $3.75 to $15.00 —bestsellers that are yours now for as little as 50¢ to $2.95!

The catalog gives you a great opportunity to build your own private library at huge savings!

So don't delay any longer—send us your name and address and 10¢ (to help defray postage and handling costs).